I0632739

Love Walked In

Aspiring Love Collection - Volume 2

Wanda B. Campbell ~ Linda Leigh Hargrove
Patricia A. Bridewell ~ Alicia Fleming
T.A. Beasley ~ Jeanette Hill
Annie Johnson ~ Tyora Moody

Tymm Publishing LLC
Columbia, SC

Love Walked In
Aspiring Love Collection: Volume 2

Copyright © 2019 by Tymm Publishing LLC

Paperback ISBN: 978-1-7336967-4-6
Ebook ISBN: 978-1-7336967-5-3

Published by Tymm Publishing LLC
701 Gervais Street, Suite 150-185
Columbia, SC 29201
www.tymmpublishing.com

Cover Design: TywebbinCreations.com
Editing: Felicia Murrell

Dedication

For those seeking true love or still healing from a broken heart, keep your eyes open. We never know who God has destined to walk through the doors of our heart.

Acknowledgements

This anthology includes stories from both veteran and first-time authors, all passionately sharing their love of romance through their stories. *Love Walked In* would not exist without the contributions of the following authors: Wanda B. Campbell, Linda Leigh Hargrove, Patricia A. Bridewell, Alicia Fleming, T.A. Beasley, Jeanette Hill and Annie Johnson. We want to express a huge thanks to Felicia Murrell for her patient editing of each co-author's short story. We hope each story leaves the reader with a smile.

Table of Contents

Listing of Short Stories

Eyes Wide Shut by **Wanda B. Campbell**

Determined to make up for wasted time spent chasing Hollywood dreams, Lexi Turner is focused on school and building her business, but not much else. With her desire for companionship hidden underneath physical and emotional scars from the past, Lexi successfully rebuffs attention from the opposite sex and works her plan toward independence. That is, until Felix the Clown shows up in the nick of time and saves the day, forcing Lexi to unpack her emotional baggage. Will persistence, patience, and blue clown shoes be enough to open her heart and eyes to what's right in front of her?

Trouble in Chow Town by **Linda Leigh Hargrove**

After years of hard work, Georgetta "Georgie" Turner is finally at a good place in her career as a Raleigh, North Carolina, detective but something's missing. Then, like a cool breeze on a hot day, Dr. Shawn Fields walks back into Georgie's life. Just when she thinks their chance meeting is a sign from above, trouble starts brewing in a racially-charged part of the city called Chow Town. There's always trouble in Chow Town, but Detective Turner is the woman for the job. Will fine Dr. Fields be there when she's done saving the day?

Love Won't Let Me Wait by **Patricia A. Bridewell**

Jamila Parker's rise to gospel recording artist is a few weeks away. Singing in a Stellar-Award winning church choir and a gospel group exceeds all expectations except one — a man who truly loves her. When a jealous ex-boyfriend begins stalking and making threats, Jamila's emotions shatter. In walks Nolan Spencer, the new minister of music who spins her mind from fantasy to reality. He is everything she has ever wanted, but is he real? Will their romance continue to flourish when Nolan's secret past is exposed, or will the chaos rip them apart?

Unlikely Companions by Alicia Fleming

Eden is a very successful businesswoman and entrepreneur who has put her love life on hold to grow her business and secure her future. Living her best life, she has it all — a men's designer clothing store, limousine service and real estate ventures. Until one night, a life-threatening emergency exposes something she doesn't have. Companionship. When a friend from the past saves her life, Eden wrestles with love? Is she infatuated with her old friend because he performed an act of heroism or does she truly have feelings for him? Will Eden make room in her best life for love?

The Gala Replacement by T.A. Beasley

Mia Stone is tired of her mother trying to match her with ego driven men. When Mia's mother announced she has the perfect date to take her to the annual gala, Mia thinks fast telling her mother she already has a date. What was she thinking lying to her mother? Will she ever find a date in time?

When the Past Comes Calling by Jeanette Hill

Widowed and over sixty, Ruth Willis isn't happy with her life. She feels like a fifth wheel in her son's home. Her only choice? Join the local straw hat and sensible shoes wearing, disease comparing garden club. But Ruth's options expand when a chance encounter with an old high school crush leads to a budding romance.

Empowered by new love, Ruth considers more opportunities to assert her newfound independence, until a devastating blow causes her to doubt herself. Maybe her son is right. Maybe there is an expiration date on love. Is it possible to be too old for a new love?

Reunited by Annie Johnson

Miranda's marriage to Troy was the kind dreams are made of – whimsical and wonderful. Right up until the day he left her suddenly and unexpected. With nothing to keep her in the windy city of Chicago, she accepts a friend's offer to headline at her jazz dinner club in Paris, France. Miranda adjusts beautifully to life in Paris living out her lifelong dream of becoming a jazz performer. Until Troy shows up, as suddenly and unexpectedly as he left, at one of her performances. Will Miranda be able to forgive Troy? Can she trust a man who disappeared or will their love stand the test of time? Will Miranda relive or worse nightmare or will her and Troy be reunited?

Southern Delights by Tyora Moody

Nia Michaels is an author who's currently experiencing writer's block. Determined to send her next novel by the deadline, she struggles for inspiration. Her own love life certainly doesn't reflect the sweet romance stories she's grown accustomed to reading and writing. When a man walks inside *Southern Delights Cafe*, catching Nia's eye, she's delighted to find the perfect male character for her novel. She sure wouldn't mind getting to know him for herself too.

Eyes Wide Shut
Wanda B. Campbell

"You want me to do what?" Lexi knew both her tone and her body language conveyed she considered her new client's request ludicrous, but she couldn't help it. As an up and coming professional party planner, she mastered creating special birthday parties for children on all types of budgets, but this request was over the top. After adjusting her neck, Lexi rephrased her objection. "Mrs. Adams—"

"It's Ms. Adams," her client corrected.

Lexi cleared her throat. "I'm sorry, Ms. Adams, I'm not sure an outdoor white linen party is appropriate for a five-year-old."

"It will be way too cute. I saw it on celebrity reality TV the other night." Tri-colored acrylic nails waved rhythmically in Lexi's face as the diva described the affair she wanted to re-create for her soon to be five-year-old. "I went online and found a white linen suit in his size with a hat and a cane and these white loafers. I want white dishes, white napkins, and white chair covers. The girls can wear white linen dresses and hats. And..."

Lexi zoned in and out while the excited mother presented her ridiculous ideas until she heard the word "menu". Most five-year-olds enjoyed pizza or hot dogs on their birthday. Surely, the mother would realize white linen would be disastrous with pizza sauce and ketchup.

"I want those cute cucumber sandwiches and a cheese tray with the cheese cut into shapes, numbers, and letters. This way, the kids can learn while they eat. For dessert, I want little white cake pops." Her hands waved in the air. "Oh! And sparkling bottled water. Normally, I would serve regular water, but since this is a special occasion, I'll bring out the bubbly."

Can you bring out some common sense? Lexi shook the thought away. As wacky as this woman was, Lexi needed the business. Being an entrepreneur of less than a year, and a college student, didn't afford her the option of turning down clients for the sole reason of foolish and inappropriate party themes for kindergarteners. She needed the money. The deposit would be enough for a down payment on a winter break trip with her bffs to Mexico. She'd have Ms. Reality TV sign a waiver releasing her of any liability for stained clothing or bored children. She manufactured a smile and stroked the keyboard on her laptop. "What's the date and location of the event?"

"July seventeenth, and I have an appointment at the Dunsmuir House this afternoon."

The historical home was totally inappropriate for a group of five-year-olds. There wasn't anywhere for the children to run free and play and parking was almost nonexistent, but Lexi's fingers kept moving. "How many total guests are you expecting?"

Ms. Reality TV tapped her nail tips rhythmically. "Hmmm, with family and his classmates, I'm thinking around fifty people."

"What games and activities would you like for the children?"

"I want the works!"

Lexi's fingers slowed. "The works?"

Ms. Adams used her fingers to count her wishes. "I want a white inflatable jumpy gym. A magic show. A balloon artist and a clown. Oh, and face painting."

Lexi's eyebrows narrowed, but her fingers kept moving.

"And don't forget, live music."

"And what's your budget?"

Ms. Adams beamed. "Money is no problem. I have five hundred dollars set aside for my baby's big day."

Lexi's fingers ceased movement as the possibility of spending a week on the beach in Cancun vanished. She'd been here before. Reality television supposedly portrayed a typical day in the life of celebrities. From Lexi's perspective and personal experience, it created unrealistic expectations for wanna be stars and average people living above their means. To recreate the social event Ms. Adams had seen on television would cost nearly four times as much in addition to the venue and food.

Lexi cleared her throat and spoke slowly. "Ms. Adams, a successful white linen party for any age group will require a more *robust* budget." She hoped Ms. Adams would catch her meaning by the emphasis she placed on robust. "Is your budget expandable?"

The woman's smile vanished. "How expandable? I may be able to come up with another three hundred dollars, maybe. But that's it."

Time for a reality check. Lexi closed her laptop and opened the folder containing services and fee schedules. Thanks to America's obsession with following celebrities through every aspect of their daily lives, these teaching moments were becoming more common than she cared for.

Lexi spent the next twenty minutes explaining the details.

"So, Ms. Adams, with the venue, entertainment, food, and my fee, this is a more realistic budget." Lexi underlined the figure in red.

Ms. Adams shrieked.

"Keep in mind, white linen parties aren't usually given for five-year-olds. We could plan something more age appropriate within your budget, if you'd like." Lexi extended the lifeline, although she doubted Ms. Adams would take it.

"That is way too much money! Do I look rich to you?" Ms. Adams stood and went on a tangent in the middle of Starbucks. "This is why I don't do business with Black people. Y'all prices are too high. You ain't all that, holding meetings in Starbucks instead of an office. I'm going to find me a real party planner like David Tutera. He knows what he's doing."

Without feeling embarrassed, Lexi gathered her belongings into her rolling briefcase and started for the exit. She'd heard it all before. Ms. Adams might live in a fantasy world, but Lexi didn't. And if she hurried, she could spend some time in the school library, researching her anthropology project.

"Good evening, beautiful."

Lexi heard the greeting each time she entered the building that housed Berkeley City College. The voice belonged to the security guard stationed behind the desk, but that's about all she knew. In the two years she'd been pursuing an associate's degree in hospitality, she never had time to notice the face that housed the voice or even acknowledge the compliment. Not that she would want to anyway. At twenty-six, and lacking a stable job with benefits, Lexi was determined to make up for the years after high school she'd wasted partying and chasing fame. With stars in her eyes, she'd moved to Los Angeles in hopes of making a career as a movie extra. The fantasy lasted all of sixty days, but pride prevented her from returning home and admitting to her family she'd made a mistake. Lexi was reared in a sheltered Christian home, and she was on a mission to experience the fun she'd missed while attending youth group. Her ambitious quest lasted four years, connecting her with seedy crowds that nearly swallowed her into a sex-trafficking ring before she called home for help. Since escaping from the movie producer/pimp, Lexi wore a mental chastity belt when it came to men and relationships. She wasn't hoping or praying for God to send her a Boaz.

"Have a good class," the voice faded as she continued up the steps after flashing her student I.D. She didn't stop until she reached her Intermediate Algebra class on the fourth floor.

"Yes!" Lexi was delighted to find the classroom empty. For at least thirty minutes, she'd have the room to herself and time to finalize the arrangements for her client's seven-year-old twin boys' birthday party on Saturday. Both parents were lawyers and had ordered and paid for the works - jumpies and a trampoline, a clown, mural painting, cookie decoration station, and a mini rock-climbing wall in addition to three food stations for kids. The success of this event could open the door to a flood of regular upscale clients, nullifying the earlier dis by Ms. Adams.

With laptop open and phone in hand, Lexi went down her checklist confirming start and stop times. Her final call was to the clown, her big brother, Jamal.

"Hey, dude, just confirming for Saturday at 2:00."

"Hey, how is my favorite college student doing?" His voice always conveyed how proud he was of her for having the courage to return to school, and his support meant more than she could express after almost losing him to an assault last year.

"I'm great, really looking forward to Saturday."

"Why? What's up?"

She looked up at the wall clock. "Stop playing, you know you're playing Rudy the Clown at my event this weekend. I just wanted to make sure you don't operate on CP time, this is a huge opportunity. And, I really appreciate you helping me again."

To help her cut cost, her brother often played Rudy the Clown at her kid parties.

"Um, I... Um—"

His stalling sent her into panic. "What?"

"Aw, Sis, I totally forgot to mark my calendar. I'm taking Kaymar to Monterey this weekend. We're leaving Friday morning. I got two rooms right on the beach and tickets to the Monterey Bay Aquarium."

"Jamal Turner, you are the most organized person I know," she screamed into the phone. "How could you let this happen?"

"I'm sorry, but I've been so busy with work and the youth group, the date slipped my mind."

"Let's not forget love," Lexi interrupted. "If you weren't so busy chasing Kaymar, you would have remembered. If I'd known love would cause you to kick me to the curb, I wouldn't have encouraged you to pursue her."

"Come on, Lexi. That's not fair."

It wasn't fair. After a disastrous marriage and a near death experience, her brother deserved some happiness, and she really did like Kaymar. Unlike his first wife,

Kaymar cherished Jamal for who he was and not for what material things he could offer.

"Be nice, she's going to be your sister-in-law someday."

"Yeah, yeah. Someday, but I need a clown on Saturday. Wait, are you proposing this weekend?"

"Maybe. What I will say is my baby has been working very hard lately and needs a change of scenery."

"And I need a clown! How am I supposed to find a reasonable clown on such short notice?"

"Since this is my fault, if you find someone, I'll cover their fee. I know how important this is for you."

"I'll hold you to that, loverboy. I have to go. Have fun. Love you." No matter how frustrated she was, Lexi always ended every call with love. Her experience had taught her never to take family or life for granted. In the few minutes left before the start of class, she searched the Internet for a clown and prayed for a miracle.

Lexi paced the lobby of the warehouse waiting for the new vendor to arrive, she checked and rechecked the time on her cell phone. Felix from *Clownin' Around* should have arrived fifteen minutes ago. When she booked the company three days ago, she stressed the need for promptness and was assured Felix the Clown would be there dressed and ready thirty minutes early. Since this was a new vendor and to ensure the birthday bash remained on schedule, the time Lexi gave them was thirty minutes prior to the actual performance time. Even with trickery, she was on the verge of creating a bad reputation for her budding business. This was the last time she would use *Clownin' Around.* She checked her clipboard for options to rearrange the schedule of events.

With thirty-five out of forty-five kids showing up, she had very little room for adjustments. So far, the kids were having a good time and the parents seemed pleased, but all that could change with dead space.

"I'm going to kill Jamal for this." She stomped out the front door to check the parking lot. After pacing the length of the building, her head jerked when she heard an engine roar and tires screech. The sounds belonged to a black Dodge Charger parking at the end of the front aisle. Her head shook in disgust. She hated when people sped through parking lots as if they were on a speedway. Before she could turn away, the driver's door opened and bright blue and red clown shoes hit the pavement.

"It's about time." She started toward him but stopped dead in her tracks when a six-foot plus frame emerged. In seconds, Lexi inspected Felix the Clown from the bottom up. Black clown pants with green suspenders that seem to go on forever. The pants were baggy, as they should be, but failed to camouflage muscular thighs. Perfectly defined biceps bulged from underneath the sleeves of a white shirt affixed with yellow, blue, and green buttons topped with a red bowtie. They flexed as he donned the black, red and blue checkered jacket. White gloves covered his hands. His facial features were hidden behind white face paint, a red nose and red lipstick, and a red wig covered his hair. He looked down at a piece of paper, and then discarded it inside the vehicle. After retrieving a black bag from the back seat, Felix the Clown started toward the building.

"Oh my," Lexi whispered. Maybe it was the shoes, but she had never seen a clown, or any man for that matter, with a gait as sexy as Felix the Clown. His stride had a slip dip, almost like a limp then smoothed out. He walked with confidence. Previous experience taught her not to base a man's character on his physical appearance, but this clown was like none she'd ever seen. Even hidden behind clown makeup, Felix was fine. If he impressed the kids half as much, the party would be a success.

Lord, help me. I'm lusting after a clown. Lexi shook her head to clear it. Attractive or not, business was business and Felix the Clown was late. "You must be Felix. I was expecting you twenty minutes ago." An extended hand accompanied the greeting/reprimand.

Dark brown eyes stared back. His mouth opened and closed several times before asking, "Are you Lexi?"

"Yes, and you are late."

"I'm sorry. There was an accident. I had—"

"It doesn't matter why you're late, just do a great job. You're on in fifteen minutes." She felt like his dark brown eyes were studying her.

"Since you're paying," his voice deepened, "your wish is my command."

My wish is that you stop looking at me like that. Lexi returned his stare, grateful that he couldn't read her mind, and then went back inside to the party. The squeak of his blue and red clown shoes confirmed he followed.

"The clown is finally here," she informed her assistant, Olivia, who was actually her mother.

Olivia glanced at the clown. "Good, now you can stop worrying. I doubt if the kids would even miss the clown, considering how much fun they're having in the jumping gym and on the trampoline."

Lexi's back was to Felix, but she could feel him watching. She resisted the urge to turn around. "Their parents might, and I need referrals. I'm trying to build a business, a top-notch business, that delivers as promised on time."

"I won't let you down." Felix's deep voice caused both women to jerk their head in his direction. "Once again,

I'm sorry about being late, but I promise to do a great job."

His words didn't alleviate her anxiety. The last man who had vowed never to let her down offered her up as a toy to his drug induced friends. There were only three men Lexi trusted to keep their word, and Felix the Clown wasn't one of them. But his confidence expressed how seriously he took his job, and she liked that.

"Thank you." Lexi quickly turned away to keep from staring at him. The only visible facial characteristic were his dark brown eyes, and the way they bore into her unnerved her. "My assistant, Olivia will let you know when it's time to go on." Lexi left to check on the food stations.

"He's good."

Lexi jumped at Olivia's assessment of Felix the Clown. She'd been so engrossed in the performance, she was oblivious to her mother's approach. Felix was good. He did it all and looked good while doing it. Lexi had seen many clowns perform, but not once had she considered juggling and tumbling sexy. Nor had she laughed so much at kiddie jokes. But then, no other clown sounded sexy speaking in falsetto either. Once Felix stepped on stage, he transformed into an entertainer, engaging both parents and children.

"Yeah, he is pretty good. I might use him again in a crunch." Lexi downplayed her attraction. This was business. She no longer lived in a fantasy world and had given up fairytales when her rich prince turned into a monster. She had a permanent two-inch scar on her left cheek as a reminder, dreams do not always come true. The attraction to Felix was fleeting, she decided.

"Why don't you contract with him on a regular basis? I'm sure Jamal won't mind."

"I'll think about it." Her mother's suggestion was a good one, but Lexi wouldn't follow through.

"Don't think too long. A man, I mean, a clown like that won't be available forever."

"Mama!"

"Mama nothing. I saw how he was gawking at you. And you're practically salivating. You know he goes to church."

She hated when her mother was right but refused to give her the satisfaction. "Ms. Turner, this is business. If I'm salivating, it's over new business opportunities. And just how do you know he attends church?"

"I asked him. He's not married, but has a little girl, thirteen-years-old. That's how he started clowning; his daughter loved clowns when she was younger."

"What did you do, interview him the second I turned my back?"

"Sure did," Olivia shrugged, "and he passed with flying colors."

Lexi chuckled but held her resolve. "Thanks for being who you are, Mama, but it's just business for me."

Her mom sighed in resignation. "If you say so."

Lexi leaned against her mother as Felix went into his grand finale of singing, dancing, and tumbling. By the last flip, the children, parents, and Lexi were applauding and cheering.

"That was fantastic!" Lexi told Felix the Clown when he joined her and Olivia. "You were true to your word. You did not let me down."

"Thank you." The deep voice was back. "Glad I could help you out. Much success with your business."

"You're welcome, Felix. It is Felix, right?"

His red lips parted into a smile. "Actually, it's Logan. My name is Logan Davis. And I assume Lexi is short for Alexis?"

Lexi swallowed to lubricate her suddenly parched throat. Those eyes were examining her again. "No. Alexandria. My real name is Alexandria Turner."

"Hmm," Olivia moaned.

"Alexandria... You have a beautiful name."

Lexi shook her head. Why had she told the man her real name? She hated her name, but it sounded lovely rolling off his lips. She had to get away from him and away from her mother's snickering. "Thank you, Logan, it was nice meeting you. And thanks again for accepting on such short notice. As agreed, the balance of your invoice will be paid electronically." She turned to walk away, thinking she had successfully dismissed him.

Her mom had other plans. "Logan, if you're not in a hurry, I could use some help loading the van."

"No problem. Give me a minute to run to the car and change my shoes, and I'm all yours." Logan looked at Lexi. "I'll be right back." He disappeared before Lexi could object.

"Mama, what are you doing? You know we don't need help."

"*Alexandria*," she laughed, "calm down. I'll keep him occupied while you do your thing."

Lexi glanced at her watch. She didn't have time to lecture her mother in her obvious game of matchmaking. "I have to go, but remember, I am not interested."

"I know, *Alexandria*."

Lexi ignored her mother's laughter and concentrated on her clients. While keeping the remaining activities on schedule for the next hour, she'd spot her mother and Logan talking and packing away used supplies. She couldn't imagine what sales pitch her mother was making, but Lexi secretly enjoyed the view of his biceps now that he'd removed his jacket. She also caught him staring at her a few times, maybe he was staring at her scar. She wasn't a troll, but the scar had made her less attractive in her eyes. For a while, she tried camouflaging it with makeup, and when that failed, she accepted the memorial scar as a testimony of God's miraculous deliverance. Still, there were times being self-conscious reared its ugly head, and she'd hide the scar behind a scarf or head wrap. Though neither was an option today.

More than once, she found herself wondering what Logan looked like underneath the makeup, and then scolded herself for having such a thought. It didn't matter. If she were to see him again, it would be for clown services only.

"Yes!" Lexi thrust her hands in the air after the last guest exited the warehouse. "Thank you, Jesus!" Several parents had asked for her business card, and three tentatively booked her services for the fall season. *Sweet Memories by Lexi* was on the map. She skipped over to where Logan and her mother were chatting and shared the good news.

"I told you not to worry," her mother said. "God has blessed you with the creativity and organizational skills to do the job. I'm just here to help out where I can."

"I appreciate you, Mama." And with the new business, I can fire you and hire someone who will stay out my personal business. Lexi smiled.

"Congratulations, Alexandria."

Lexi knew he was standing there, but Logan's voice made her pulse race. She forced her eyes to meet his. "Thanks." Her fingers instinctively rested on the left side of her face. "Perhaps we will do business again, and you can call me Lexi."

"But Alexandria is more beautiful."

No, I didn't just blush! Lexi stepped back and reached for her briefcase. "I need to gather my belongings and sign out with the manager."

"Everything is already in the van. Logan and I took care of everything while you chatted with your clients. Wait until I tell Jamal how his memory lapse blessed you today, *Alexandria*." Olivia laughed out the door.

"I'll have to thank your brother as well," Logan added.

Lexi became suspicious. Was her brother in cahoots with her mother? She folded her arms. "How do you know Jamal?"

"I don't. Your mother explained how his cancellation opened the door for me to officially meet you. It appears Jamal blessed both of us today."

"I see." Lexi wasn't convinced their meeting was happenstance, but it didn't matter. She had accomplished her goal. "Well, I'm out of here." She started for the door, but Logan caught up with her at the van.

"Alexandria, can I call you sometime?"

Part of her wanted to scream yes, but her protective wall wouldn't allow it. "For what? If I need your services, I'll call you." Lexi regretted the words the second he turned and walked away. He probably wasn't a bad guy, but she couldn't take the chance to find out. She climbed into the van, but before she ignited the engine, Logan was at her window.

"Here's my cell number in case you ever need my services again or just want to talk. I would love to get to know who you are when you're not working or attending school. And, if your schedule permits, perhaps you'll let me take you on a date."

"Girl, he's serious," her mother offered from the passenger seat.

Logan was serious, but Lexi didn't even know who she was aside from work and school. And, even if she was interested, she couldn't tell him what she didn't know. "There's not much to know," she whispered after a pronounced pause.

The piece of a paper slipped from his extended hand and onto her lap. "Let me be the judge of that." Then he was gone.

Lexi never saw the digits on paper. Her mother took the liberty of texting Logan's number to Lexi's phone.

Sunday morning service was Lexi's favorite worship time. As a teen, she hated spending every Sunday in church and fellowshipping with the saints afterward. After her ordeal in Los Angeles, she'd gained an appreciation for the household of faith. Although sometimes overbearing, the saints always held her best interest at heart and loved her despite her many faults. Her church family welcomed her back with open arms and supported her business by contracting her services for events. More than one mother thought she'd make the perfect wife for their son, grandson, or nephew, but Lexi wasn't interested in a relationship. She'd forgiven herself for making a bad decision, but the fear of trusting a man again paralyzed her. And if she were completely honest, she considered herself damaged goods.

This Sunday, Lexi didn't leave service feeling rejuvenated as normal, and she couldn't identify why. All of the elements were there. Praise and worship was powerful, the choir was energetic, and the sermon was uplifting. Like always, she poured her heart out during prayer, but today, she didn't feel content. By the time dinner rolled around, she accepted the cause of her unease.

As she suspected, Jamal returned from Monterey with a fiancée. Kaymar glowed as she showed off her engagement ring. Free to love again, Jamal's laughter was back – his heart had healed from betrayal. Lexi was truly happy for her brother, she knew the tears that wouldn't stop falling were from a place of longing deep inside of her. She desired what Jamal and Kaymar had found, and that reality overwhelmed her. She went to her bedroom in search of comfort, but she was still crying when Jamal knocked on the door and entered.

"Are you okay?"

Lexi sat up on the bed and sniffled. She tried to compose herself, but it was useless to put up a front with Jamal. He knew her too well.

"I was expecting you to scream, 'I knew it!', not run in here and hide. I hope you're happy for me."

"Of course I'm happy for you. You know I never liked your first wife, but I love Kaymar. It's just that being happy for you has opened my eyes to how pathetic my life is."

Her big brother placed his arm around her shoulder, and she rested her head against him.

"Your life can't be any more pathetic than mine was after the divorce. I thought my chance for love had passed. Then, I got assaulted and found my soulmate. Kaymar loves and accepts me for who I am, and she respects me. She enhances my life. I truly love her with my whole heart."

Lexi bobbed her head. "I know, I can tell. I've never seen you this happy."

"Happiness is waiting for you too, if you get over your fear of being hurt again." She shook her head against his shoulder. "Ma told me you met someone yesterday. Logan?"

Lexi raised her head and glared at her brother. "Exactly what do you know about Felix the Clown?"

Jamal waved his hands in defense. "I promise, I am not matchmaking. I really did mess up my schedule. I have never met this clown."

They shared a laugh.

"Okay, but if I find out otherwise..."

"Seriously, Lexi, give him a chance. Pray about it first but be open to what God says. And if he turns out to be a jerk, I'll beat him up."

"I'm sure you will. Now, get out of my room." She pointed toward the door. "I'll be out in a minute."

Jamal nodded and stood to his feet.

"And, bro," Lexi watched as her brother turned back to look at her, "congratulations!"

He smiled and closed the door behind him.

Lexi prayed, and two hours later, she stepped out of her comfort zone. The phone rang twice before a young female answered.

Lexi started to hang up, maybe her mother transcribed the number wrong. "Hello, is Logan available?"

"Just a moment, please. Daddy, telephone."

Lexi relaxed. She'd forgotten Logan had a daughter. *Better a daughter than a girlfriend.*

"Hello."

Mentally, she merged his melodic phone voice with a visual picture and moaned.

"Hello, is someone there?"

She cleared her throat. "Hi, Logan, it's me, Lexi from yesterday at the party. You gave me your number, and well... I um... I don't mean to bother you. I—"

"Hello, Alexandria. I'm glad you called."

He had stopped her from sounding like an idiot, now what? "Well, I just wanted to say how much I enjoyed you yesterday."

"Alexandria, it's okay to say you were thinking about me. You've been on my mind for a while."

"Really?"

"Since the first time I saw you, I've wanted a conversation with you."

"Well, you got that and more."

"Hold a minute." She waited as he gave instructions to his daughter. "Now, where were we?"

"What's your daughter's name?" Lexi figured that was a safe subject. "Does she live with you?"

"My little princess' name is Tiana. Her mother and I share custody."

"Little? Your daughter is thirteen, almost a teenager. She'll be ready for dating in a few years."

"Don't remind me, but she will always be my baby." His voice softened as he spoke, love for his daughter evident. "Good thing I'm not thirty yet. I'll still be in prime shape to handle any knucklehead wanting to date my baby."

Lexi did the math in her head. "So, you had your daughter young? Uh, not that it's any of my business."

"I don't mind you asking. I'm not ashamed of my past. Tiana was born my junior year of high school. Her mother and I were way too young for marriage, and discovered after a couple of years, we made better parents than partners once the high school crush wore off. We're great at co-parenting. She's married with more children."

So, no baby mama drama. That's one point. "I appreciate you being willing to share." Not sure how to direct the conversation, Lexi relied on the familiar. "So, is Felix the Clown your full-time gig?"

His jovial laughter surprised her. "Are you kidding? I only let Felix out occasionally on weekends. I'd never be able to support a child, and someday a wife, on a clown's salary. My day job is much more financially stable and serious. Sometimes, too serious, and since Tiana has outgrown clowns, transforming into Felix helps me relieve stress."

Lexi wanted to ask about his line of work but decided to let him take the lead and disclose what he felt necessary. In addition to learning about his family dynamics, Lexi learned his basic likes and dislikes in food, cars, movies, and hobbies. Christianity wasn't a novelty, but the foundation on which he modeled his life. She laughed at the dry sense of humor in which he shared his experiences. Before she knew it, an hour had passed.

"So how does Alexandria relieve stress? What do you do to relax?"

Her laughter ceased as she faced another truth. "I'll relax after I finish school." She shifted gears again. "So, when can I see you without the makeup?"

"When would you like to?"

Lexi didn't want to sound anxious, but the mystery was killing her. Not that Logan had to be a '10', because she didn't consider herself one, but cute would be nice just in case something developed between them. "Do you have a social media page? I could check there."

"And how would you know it's the real me? You can be whomever you want on the Internet." Lexi hadn't thought of that. "I have a page, but I don't use my real name. I think a face-to-face meeting would be better. Say, dinner and a movie?"

"Um, well, I'm not— "

"It's okay, Alexandria. I know it took a lot for you to make this phone call. I'll take what I can get, no pressure."

Lexi's phone chimed, alerting her to a text message.

"That's me sending you a picture."

"Really? I can't wait to see you," she squealed before sobering. "I mean, I'm curious."

"If you'd only look, you could see me every day."

His voice was more serious than she thought necessary, but she didn't address his comment. "Hold on, let me see what you're working with before I agree to being seen in public with you." She giggled and tapped the message icon, waiting for his photo to download. A feeling she hadn't felt in years stirred against her will, but she welcomed the excitement. Then she gasped, and Logan roared with merriment.

"That was dirty. How could you play me like that?" The body in the photo was him wearing jeans and a muscle shirt, but the head was photoshopped with Felix the Clown's face. "Why did you do that?"

"You have to admit it's funny, and because I really want you to see me in person. Besides, you've just given me proof that you're interested in me for more than just business."

Lexi's jaw moved to deny the truth, but she let her guard down and somewhat gave into the moment. "You might be good for a free meal and a movie. When would you like to go?"

"Hold on." Through muffled sounds, Lexi heard Logan speaking with his daughter. "Sweetheart, I need to take Tiana home. She has school in the morning. Perhaps we can get together tomorrow after your class?"

To her surprise, Lexi wasn't ready to end the conversation. "*Sweetheart*? That's a little presumptuous, don't you think?"

He didn't take the bait. "You're right. Chances are you won't see me tomorrow either. At any rate, I've locked your number in my phone, so I'll call you tomorrow. Oh, Alexandria," he added, before disconnecting, "don't think I didn't notice you avoided giving up any information about yourself, but tomorrow is another day. Good night."

Lexi stared at the phone long after the call ended. She wanted more of Logan Davis. "Big bro, I hope you're right, or I'm in trouble."

Lexi walked with a new stride after depositing the final payment from Saturday's party. Her life was finally changing for the better and feeling like a failure for wasting her life on a fantasy was lifting. Three more classes and the first degree would be under her belt. Her family was proud of her, and now Lexi was starting to feel proud of herself. While waiting for the light to change, she studied her reflection in the glass building on the corner. Her skirt looked good with the knee-high boots she'd purchased with the tip her clients had given her. Her shoulder-length hair moved with the light breeze, basking in the sunshine. Life was so good, she decided to treat herself to a scoop of ice cream before class. The simple pleasure put her behind schedule. She ran into the building with only five minutes to spare.

"Hello, beautiful."

She heard the tired greeting, but like always, Lexi rushed past the security station with her student I.D. held out in route to the elevator. She made it to the fourth floor just before the teacher greeted the class. Instead of concentrating on the lecture about storms, Lexi's thoughts drifted to Logan. He had said he would call and set up their date, but so far, she hadn't heard from him. Not even a text message. Not wanting to give the impression she was desperate, she refused to call him. True, she enjoyed his conversation and she liked him, but she would never chase a man again. Even still, she was disappointed when he hadn't contacted her by the end of class. "Oh, well, I can take myself on a date," she mumbled, after checking her cell phone while waiting for the elevator.

"Have a good day," the security guard saluted students as they exited the building. Lexi's response was to stick her earbuds in and sway out the door.

The trek back to the BART station was heavier than the trek to school. The sky was still clear and the weather warm, but now she was aware of the many couples walking along the sidewalk. Black, white, Latino, Asian, and mixed couples maintaining physical contact presented another reality check. She leaned against a cement wall with her arms wrapped around her body, observing others receiving the affection she wanted. Remembering the last time her need was met, she massaged the scar on her left cheek and quickly sobered. "Never again," she mumbled, walking toward the station.

Later that night, her phone rang just as she was finishing up some more anthropology research. She started not to answer.

Instead of saying 'hello', she snapped, "It's a good thing I don't have to depend on you for food."

"Aw, you missed me. That's so sweet."

As much as she wanted to have an attitude with Logan, his laughter and truth made her smile. "Whatever." She smacked her lips to keep from giggling. "You didn't have to stand me up, and you could have called or text."

"You're right, I should have sent you a text once I realized today wasn't a good day. I'll do better next time."

"How do you know there's going to be a next time?"

"Because you like talking to me. Now tell me, how was your day?"

Without hesitation, Lexi recapped her day right down to the new boots, she even sent him a picture. When she finished, she moved on to politics, then music, and every other subject that came to mind.

Over the next two weeks, they spent hours on the phone each evening. Logan shared childhood and life experiences, his failures and lessons learned, his desire to be a good father and Christ-follower, what he desired in a relationship. Lexi stuck to what she considered safe subjects: her family, school, the business, and church.

Each time they planned to meet, Logan backed out for one reason or another. During the week, work, which he often described as public safety, was the reason. His weekends alternated between Tiana and family obligations, and Lexi had clients to attend to. No matter what was going on, they talked and/or texted daily. The more they talked, the more Lexi lowered her defenses, a little. She was using their friendship as a safe way to fill the void of companionship without emotional or physical strings attached, and he offered her safe companionship. At least, that's how she justified the relationship to her mother, who constantly pestered her for updates. But, she liked him more than she wanted to admit,

"Tiana wants to know if you're my girlfriend," Logan said when he answered the phone tonight. "She says we've been spending a lot of time together on the phone."

Though the question took Lexi by surprise, a smile instantly spread across her face. "No, I will not have a boyfriend whose face I've never seen."

"Hopefully, that will change real soon. I've waited a long time for you to see me."

"I can't wait." She switched into an update about her latest client but noticed Logan didn't comment or ask questions. "What's up? Why are you so quiet?"

"Honestly?"

"Of course. Did something happen at work?"

"No, at least not what I want to happen."

"Well, what's up?"

Is he seeing someone?

"Alexandria, we have been talking every day, and I am no closer to knowing who you are than I was two weeks ago. I am an open book. You talk to me about everything except who you are. Whenever you come close to opening up, you shut down. Other than the business, what are your dreams? What makes you sad or happy? What are you passionate about? What characteristics do you desire in a man? Do you plan to marry and have children? Do you even like children? Sweetheart, please, tell me who you are. I'll take anything."

Lexi shook her head as if he could see her. "I can't," she whispered.

"Why?"

She rubbed her left cheek. "Because the last man I shared my dreams with tried to destroy them by slashing my face, among other things."

"I understand now," he said after a long pause. "So, you refuse to open up to me because of what some animal did?"

"That's pretty much it in a nutshell."

"But I'm not him."

"Maybe not, but I have to protect myself. I won't allow myself to be used by anyone ever again. Any relationship will have to be on my terms or not at all." The words didn't sound fair, but she had to say them. She'd lost too much the last time. The silence lasted so long, she wondered if he'd hung up. But she refused to call his name and give the impression her position was negotiable.

"I'm sorry you feel the need to protect yourself from me. I understand now. I don't like it, but I can respect it."

Relief washed over her. He finally got it.

"I can respect it, because I have to protect myself from you as well."

Her face twisted. "What do you mean? I haven't done anything to you."

"Alexandria, I'll be straight with you. For almost two years, I have been trying to get to know you."

She interrupted him with a chuckle. "You're going to have to come up with better game than that, considering we just met two weeks ago."

"True. We officially met two weeks ago, but I have been watching you and speaking to you since the first day I saw you walk through those glass doors without any acknowledgement from you."

What is he talking about?

"I had just about given up hope of you noticing me until I showed up as Felix. That day confirmed my suspicions about you being special and I pursued you. I was fearful, but my desire to know you outweighed that fear. It wasn't your mother's matchmaking either. I didn't tell her I'd been admiring you from afar. It was you. Your beauty. Your drive and determination."

"But—"

"Let me finish. Since that day, I have been trying to get you to *see* me, but you refuse and now I know why. You will never see me as long as your eyes are shut behind the past. I'm sorry for what happened to you, but I didn't cause your pain, and I won't pay for it either, even if I have begun to care about you."

"Now, wait just a minute. I—"

"Alexandria, I wish you well with your business and wherever life's journey may take you. I'll even pray for your success, but I won't bother you again. Goodbye."

The call ended before Lexi could process she'd been dumped without officially being in a relationship.

25

She dialed him back, but the call went straight to voicemail.

"This is all your fault!" Lexi barged into Jamal's office shortly after 9 a.m., ready to lay the blame for her emotional turmoil on him. She'd been up half the night sulking over a man – something she vowed never to do again. But here she was, too angry to admit how close Logan came to scaling the protective wall surrounding her heart.

Startled, Jamal looked up, then causally reached for his coffee and took a sip. "What's my fault?"

"Listening to your stupid advice got me dumped, and I wasn't even in a relationship. Well, not really."

"If he dumped you, that means I don't have to beat him up since you're the one who screwed up."

His smirk drove her into a temper tantrum, complete with stomping, yelling, neck rolling and wild hand waving. "Jamal Turner, you make me sick! Why does it have to be my fault? I listened to you and gave him a chance. It's not my problem if he can't accept me on my terms. He's a good guy and all, but I'm not changing for nobody. I'm not letting no one take advantage of me again! I will not allow my heart to get stomped on again." Lexi wrapped her arms protectively around her body. "Never. I won't. I can't..." Spent from her temper tantrum and all the fear and desire driving her emotions, she walked over to the window.

Jamal joined her and placed his arm around her shoulder. "You really like him?"

She rested her head against her brother. "Maybe. A little. Yes."

"Tell me about him. I know what Mama said, but I want to hear from you."

Without changing positions, she expressed everything she liked about Logan, from his dorky sense of humor to his sexy walk. "He's attentive and engaging. He encourages me with my business and school, even prays for me. He's not a user. Not once has he asked me for anything. He works hard. He's a very devoted father, the kind I would want for my children." Her head lifted. "The only negative thing I can say is, I don't know what he looks like behind that clown face."

"Would it matter what he looks like?"

Lexi thought long before she answered. "No, just as long as he's not super ugly. He's a good guy," she whispered.

Jamal squeezed her shoulder before removing his arm. "So, fear is the only reason you're disrupting my place of business first thing in the morning."

She rolled her eyes but didn't argue the truth.

He palmed her face back toward his. "Little Sis, learn to trust yourself again. Release the pain of past mistakes and listen to what your heart is telling you. If he's a good man, why make him pay for the deeds of a bad man? I've been where you are. I know how you feel. More than anything, I know you need love and have a lot of love to give. You'll never know if he's the right one if you push him away."

She pouted and swatted his hand away. "I didn't push him away."

"Yes, you did. And exactly why haven't you seen his face?"

Lexi threw her hands in the air. "With school, clients and his work schedule and family obligations, our schedules can't seem to line up."

"What about social media? He doesn't do selfies?"

"He doesn't use his real name on the Internet and won't tell me his alias. I tried to get a picture, but he wants me to see him in person." Lexi bit her lower lip. "Last night, he said something really strange."

"Like what?"

"He said he's been trying to get to know me for almost two years, but we just met two weeks ago at the party."

Jamal walked back to his desk and sat down. "Are you sure his elevator goes all the way to the top floor?"

She ignored the joke. "I'm sure. He said he wanted to meet me the first day I walked through the glass doors. I have no idea of what he's talking about. The only glass doors I enter on a regular basis are the ones at..." She gasped and slapped her forehead. "Oh my God! I am such an idiot. How did I miss that? It all makes sense now. He really does like me." Her emotions and thoughts collided filling the room with giggles. "I can't believe I didn't catch that. I am such a moron. He must think I'm a rude snob with an I.Q. of minus ten."

"I'd rate you a twenty-five."

"Shut up. I don't have time for your stand-up comedy routine." Lexi reached for her coat. "I have to get to school."

"I thought you didn't have classes on Fridays."

"Normally, I don't. But today is special, I'm the one teaching the lesson," she tied her belt and walked toward the door. "You can make up for the emotional rollercoaster you took me on this morning with a pair of boots, gray, you know the size. Macy's has a sale this weekend. Thanks. Love ya!"

For the first time ever, Lexi walked through the glass doors of Berkeley City College and didn't rush about her business. Instead, she stood back against a wall out of sight. Watching. "Nice," she whispered, then giggled. There he was standing – tall and muscular like she remembered. The uniform pants complimented him in all the right places, just like the clown costume had. His midsection was tight but bulked from the holster and firearm attached at the waist. Lexi giggled again, remembering he had referred to his line of work as public safety. His hands were big and void of jewelry. His chocolate skin was darker than she imagined, but it worked for her. His hair was cut low with an even trim. Aside from a pencil thin mustache, his face was clean. His physical attributes rated him an eight in the fine category, but combined with what Lexi knew about his character, she boosted him to just shy of a ten. He appeared to be instructing a colleague with a soft, but serious facial expression. He closed the binder. She couldn't see where he'd placed it from where she stood. His conversation ended in laughter - the roaring laughter she'd become fond of.

"I can do this." She gave herself the pep talk as fifth thoughts set in – second, third, and fourth thoughts had tortured her on the train ride over. "I like him. He's real. Stop living in the past." The mental battle repeated until he left the desk and started down the hall toward the stairs. The basement level was huge. She had to catch him. "It's now or never," she declared and took off. She reached the stairwell just as he cleared the last step.

"Hello, handsome," she called out, then started her descent, holding onto the rail but watching him.

In slow motion, it seemed, Logan turned around. The instant eye contact almost made her miss a step. Those dark brown eyes were still intense, but now she recognized gentleness. His eyes never left her as she made her way to the landing.

His arms were at his side. "May I help you?"

She glanced at his name badge. *So, Sargent Davis wants to play hard to get.* She shook her head at the irony of the situation before extending her hand.

"My name is Alexandria Turner," she stuttered.

"Hello, Ms. Turner." He offered his hand for a brief handshake. She obliged, but held on to him, mainly to keep from running away. "Is there something I can help you with?"

His warmth and scent pushed her over the edge. "Like I said, my name is Alexandria Turner. I am the youngest of three, and I admit I'm a little spoiled. Well, maybe more than a little by my father and brothers. But, it's okay, because I work really hard. I have too many dreams to count, but one of the main ones after succeeding in business is to one day move out of my parents' house and buy my own home. I enjoy singing, but I'm not very good at it. Live theater is my first love – any genre. Social injustices and suffering children make me sad and downright angry. I'm not a violent person, but I will fight to the death to protect those I love." She paused, allowing a group of students to pass, but didn't release his hand. "I'm passionate about exercise, but I'm also happiest cuddling up with a box of dark chocolate covered caramels and a good book. I have a serious boot fetish – leather boots, not pleather. I probably have fifty pair." The longer she spoke, the more his smile increased. "I like romantic comedies and old police dramas. I have seen every *Columbo* episode at least ten times. I watch *Law & Order* at least four nights a week, even while doing homework. I love children and hope to have some one day, as long as they are not as complicated as I am. As far as men go, all I want is someone who's honest, faithful, and loves me. And gives me space to be me. Oh, he has to share my faith." He squeezed her hand, and she almost lost the nerve to say the most important part. "I have a big heart. I also have emotional baggage that sometimes causes me to run in the opposite direction of my heart. I tend to be self-centered and rude." She took her free hand and encased his hand between hers. "I heard you greet me every time, but I ignored you. I am sorry. You were right, I never once bothered to see who you were. Honestly, I don't care who calls me beautiful, because I don't feel beautiful since my face is scarred. Whew," she exhaled loudly, "I can't believe I admitted that out loud."

Lexi didn't know what to think in the long intense silence that followed, and she had no idea what the next move should be. With every second, fear of her vulnerability increased, manifesting in her shaking body. He was still smiling, but now no teeth were showing. As another group of students approached, Logan nudged her forward. "Come with me?"

Lexi nodded her consent, then allowed him to lead her down the hall to a door near the emergency exit. Still holding her hand, he punched numbers on the keypad and pulled her into a room filled with wall monitors and other security equipment. The school's security command center.

"You won't get in trouble for me being in here, will you?"

"That's the least of my worries. My grandfather owns the company, I'm the boss." He moved into her personal space, still holding her hand.

"Oh," she mouthed.

"Alexandria, I want to hold you. May I?"

Lexi felt her eyes expand and her lips move. "W-what?" The stuttering was back.

"It cost you so much to do what you just did, you can't stop shaking. I just want to hold you until all the fear leaves and you're calm again. I promise, that's all. I won't hurt you."

"In that case, you may be holding me for the rest of your shift." Lexi tried to make light of the situation, determined to keep her emotions in check.

Logan snuggled Lexi against his chest. "I don't have a problem with that."

A whimper escaped when his words of prayer reached her ears. Hearing him pray for her peace relaxed her, and she finally stopped shaking. It took time, but she allowed herself to rest in his arms and receive his care until her nostrils transported her from comfort to lust. Logan smelled good, and his body was firm. His hands were generating warm friction down her back. She needed to end the embrace.

He rested his chin against her forehead. "How did you figure it out?"

She took a half-step back. *Whew! Thank you, Lord!* "It was what you said last night about the glass doors. Actually, I didn't connect the dots until about an hour ago when I was blaming my brother for you dumping me."

"So, in addition to being spoiled, you like to play the victim?" His smile only lasted for a moment. "Every time I gave up on you, divine intervention placed you back into view."

"Were you really desperately pining for me all this time?" This was too much like a fairytale.

"I went out on dates, but none of them intrigued me or captured my attention like you had." He reclaimed her personal space but didn't embrace her. "Sweetheart, can I kiss you?"

"What? Huh? Oh." Her head nodded yes, and his palms cupped her face. She closed her eyes and prayed her breath didn't stink. The warm soft pecks began at the top of her left cheek and trailed the length of her scar, and back up again, never touching her lips. Her eyes fluttered open to his intense gaze.

"You are so beautiful. Don't ever forget that."

Lexi's heart pounded. For the first time since the incident, she felt beautiful. Divine intervention had to be at work. The only way she could express her feelings was to press his face down to hers and kiss him, bypassing his cheek and going straight for his lips. He broke the kiss once she moaned but kept his arms around her.

"So, does this mean I can tell Tiana I have a girlfriend?"

She bit her lower lip, then blushed. "Yeah, you can tell your daughter you definitely have a girlfriend. Tell your mother, grandfather, friends, and the checker at the grocery store, I don't care, just make sure everybody knows you are taken."

He kissed her forehead, then pulled out his cell phone. "Let's send Tiana and your mother a selfie."

About the Author

Wanda B. Campbell resides is the San Francisco Bay Area with her family. She proudly balances the roles of wife, mother, grandmother, minister, mentor, teacher, author, public health care worker, and college student. Wanda began writing in 2006, and currently has twelve published Christian fiction novels. She has appeared on multiple best-selling lists and won various recognitions for her nontraditional edgy writing style. Wanda's passion is motivating others to fulfill their dreams and to pursue their passion.

Learn more about Wanda's work at: www.wandabcampbell.com or join her Facebook group: Wanda B. Campbell Readers and Supporters.

Love Walked In

Trouble in Chow Town
Linda Leigh Hargrove

Detective Georgie Turner pressed her forearm against the chest of the teenage boy she'd lined up along the chain-link fence. The kid, thin and tawny, wore a puffy down jacket over jeans so baggy that Georgie wondered why it had taken so long for her to catch his butt. Maybe five years was a little too long to be chasing down juvenile delinquents for the City of Raleigh. The pay stank, but the benefits ... what benefits?

She drew a deep breath and told herself that the rapid rhythm she felt in her wrist was the heartbeat of the seventeen-year-old knucklehead she had pinned against the fence and not evidence that she needed a desk job. At least the sun had warmed her body. She no longer felt the chill of the dry January air on the back of her neck.

The kid glared up at her. "You ain't got nothing on me, lady." His breath smelled of tar and nicotine with a hint of a substance not yet legalized in the state of North Carolina for non-medicinal use.

Georgie ignored the buzzing phone on her hip and leaned into the youth. Broken glass crunched underfoot as she rested the toe of her ankle boot on the boy's Nike. She knew the kid and the kid's family. Jaquan Park was his name but he went by ZuPack, called himself a rapper. His mother worked two minimum wage jobs. She smoked Pall Mall cigarettes like a chimney but she was an honest woman, struggling to make something for her two half-black, half-Korean sons. Georgie hated having to run Lilly Park's oldest boy down like a stray dog, but that was the job—keeping the peace.

She pursed her lips and studied the pupils trained on her. The boy rolled his almond-shaped eyes and turned his head away.

"Well, young Jaquan," Georgie started, "I ain't trying to have nothing on you. Five blocks, three wild alley cats, and two flying trash cans ago, all I wanted to do was talk to you about your old running partner, Bobby K." Georgie paused to study the knot swelling on her wrist from fending off one of the metal cans. With her light brown coloring, the resulting bruise was sure to be a nasty one. *Perks of the job*, she mused, then turned her attention back to the kid kissing the fence. "I'm starting to wonder what *my* partner is pulling up in the squad car right now that will make me change my mind. Maybe I would want to find *something* on you. Just in case *something* turns up on the computer. A report of three black youths involved in a recent string of break-ins."

"Man, you talking stupid. Get up off my back, lady."

Georgie pushed her face closer to the boy's but quickly turned her head at the sound someone's approach. Out of the corner of her eye, she saw the gruff bushy-eyebrowed frown of her partner, Milton Hayes.

"Just got a text from HQ. You need to radio in, Detective Turner," Hayes reported.

Georgie pushed up off the kid, sending a rippling rattle along the fence. Goodness. Had she been pressing him that hard? She took one last look at the boy before glancing down at the cell phone clipped on her belt. Two texts from HQ. She'd only felt it vibrate once. "Detective Hayes here will do his little patty finger bit on you, Jaquan. We don't wanna have to take you on a trip downtown."

"I ain't got nothing on me. I was on my way to see my girl. That's all," Jaquan protested with vehemence, uttering a word that rhymed with itch. "If you find anything on me, it's because this old white dude here planted it." The kid jabbed a finger at Hayes.

"All I wanna plant on you, kid, is a breath mint." Hayes' face broadened into a grimace. "You know the drill, Jaquan. Turn around. Hands on the fence. Feet apart. Mouth shut."

Jaquan complied but not before telling Hayes where to go. Hayes didn't respond, which was odd for him in Georgie's mind. The way her partner's bushy salt-and-pepper eyebrows met in the middle of his forehead made Georgie frown. Hayes had either found something peculiar on Jaquan or this call from HQ was a bad one. Five years with the old ex-Marine had taught her how to read his moods. The trip downtown was going to be interesting.

The short walk back to their car took Georgie's smile away. She kicked a spent needle from the curb and opened the car door. For a split second, she thought she caught a familiar aroma. Finally, her mind wrapped around the smell.

Pig feet? Who would be cooking pig feet at seven a.m. on a Monday morning?

Then she remembered the fame of the East Side: a Purina dog food processing plant across the highway. People familiar with the area called it Chow Town after the Purina dog food brand.

A window opened in a duplex three doors down, spewing the latest rap beat. Rundown brick duplexes and triplexes stretched along either side of Fenton Street as far as she could see. Gray bundles of trash huddled on every stoop as a dingy dog trotted from one gray trash can to the next. Grayness covered everything, even the sky. From the look of things, fog was rolling in from nearby Walnut Creek.

Georgie hated Raleigh's East Side, especially in winter. It was in December, five years earlier, that she had had a front-row seat to a riot. Down at the station, the old cops like Hayes called it 'that big trouble in Chow Town'. There was always some kind of trouble on the east side but that weekend was epic. Thirty-two hours of looting and fires led to several attacks on Koreans and one dead Korean shopkeeper. East Side's black population blamed the violence on injustices from the city. Not enough city funds funneled into starting black-owned businesses. Too much for Koreans, they had said. It didn't help matters that Raleigh's first Korean-American mayor seemed indifferent to the plight of East Side blacks.

Georgie had ended up having to get ten stitches to her head after confronting a group of looters. With her riot helmet knocked off, she'd hit the ground hard. Apparently making off with three boxes of Air Jordan's was worth assaulting an officer. Anger did funny things to a person. She'd seen it many times in her five years with Raleigh PD.

To Georgie, being angry at the powers-that-be was no excuse for the vicious actions of East Side's black residents. Where was their dignity, their respect for the property of others? Amid threats of a trial against her for police brutality, Georgie had testified against those charged with murdering the shop owner. The two black suspects were now serving life sentences.

She'd grown up poor too, a product of farming communities around Rocky Mount, North Carolina, an hour drive east of Raleigh, the capital city. Her mother was an evangelist, traveling from church to church, earning whatever the meager congregations took up in offerings. Her father was a paper mill worker, preaching the gospel in the pulpit of pulp and steam. To them, if a man didn't work, he shouldn't eat. "Working" up enough energy to go to the mailbox to pick up your government check was not real labor.

Georgie slipped into the cruiser's driver seat and closed the door against the noise and the stench. She reached for the palm mic on the police radio and switched to a private channel.

The sight of a black Jaguar sedan coming down Fenton toward her was a welcomed distraction. A slow smile spread across her face. Every time she saw a black Jag, her mind went to a happier time, her first semester as grad student at North Carolina Central's Criminal Justice School when she first met the handsome driver of an impeccable shiny black car. His name was Shawn Fields, or rather Dr. Shawn Fields, the newest professor in Central's Sports Science program. Back in the day, she and her sorors called him "Dr. So Fine" because he turned all the ladies' heads as he strolled across campus or swaggered through the gym. The man truly had a way with walking, like poetry in motion.

It was common for one of her girlfriends to give her a teasing jab to the rib and whisper, "There goes your boyfriend." They'd even made up a little jingle about his aloof nature toward them.

Your cold shoulder makes me sigh
This ain't dust in my eye
Don't stand and watch me grieve, walk on by

41

You don't want to see me cry
Please, fine sir, walk on by

Georgie figured he was only being polite when he tossed a casual wave in their direction. Her friends all swore he had set his cap on her after he'd attended one of her intramural basketball games.

As hoop season slipped away, the supposed relationship never materialized. And, for the two and a half years she'd spent there, Georgie had only admired him (and fantasized about him) from afar. What would a young successful prof like him want with a big country girl like her?

She hadn't seen tall muscle-bound Dr. Fields since the day of her master's defense. He'd passed her in the gym hallway the morning of her big day and tossed her a beguiling smile. "You're Georgetta Turner, right?" he'd asked, and her heart had done a happy flip despite the nerves she felt. "I know your master's committee chairperson. You'll do fine today. Praying for you."

The fact that he was a god-fearing man turned her off at first. Back then, cocky Georgetta May Turner had her sights on being the first black police chief back home in Martin County. A relationship with her Maker was not even close to being on her radar in those days, but her mother's long battle with cancer had turned Georgie's eyes on the eternal. Spending the first five years of her law enforcement career under her mother's roof had been good for their mother-daughter relationship. And even though her mother expressed some misgivings about her only daughter walking a beat instead of pounding a pulpit, the two Turner women grew close to each other and to their Savior.

On her deathbed, Mama Turner expressed one regret: Georgie had never married.

Her mother had been gone over five years, but she could still hear her words. "I love you, Georgetta."

"I love you too, Mama." Hearing Mrs. Turner's labored breathing pained Georgie. She wanted to leave her brother to endure the passing of their last living parent alone, but somehow, she'd found the courage to lean in and place her tear-stained cheeks against her mother's forehead.

"Promise me something, baby."

How could she oppose May Turner in her last hours of life? "Anything."

"Promise me you'll find a good God-loving man and settle down soon."

In that moment, Georgie let her mind replay her memories of Dr. So Fine and his black Jag. She knew from the campus rumor mill that he was a man of God, but the question was how he felt about a tall big-boned woman like her.

Half a decade later, though she had dated a few guys, Georgie was still married to her work. At least she'd been promoted to detective. She'd lost count how many times she'd wondered about fine Dr. Fields. Was he still working at North Carolina Central? And was he still unattached?

The Motorola crackled with static, pulling her back to reality.

She held the button down on the hand mic. "Turner here."

It was Betty from the chief's office telling Georgie she'd received a call from someone who claimed he was an old college friend.

"Betty, why are you telling me this right now?"

Betty cleared her throat. In her mind's eye, Georgie could see the woman's lips pursed and her real chin sticking out a little more than her other two. She looked and acted too much like a bloodhound which had to help with her job security. Georgie enjoyed yanking Betty's chain whenever she got the chance. "I knew you'd say that. That's why I saved the recording of the conversation."

"And why on earth did you do that, Betty?"

"Because, Detective Turner," she stressed the word detective as if it were a term Georgie used for her own entertainment. "The man who called is none other than Dalton O'Rear. No, wait a minute. He changed his name recently. What does he call himself now? I didn't even know you knew him. He's been in the national news so much lately, and you've said nothing to nobody."

Georgie doubted the caller was indeed Dalton O'Rear aka Ahmad Elali aka Brother Ahmad. Betty was known to be more than a little sensational, reading too much into a situation. But her curiosity was piqued. If it were indeed the man, why would he be calling Georgie? She hadn't heard from her old friend for years. That last call had been the day before Ahmad's sentencing in a rape trial. The then "Dee" O'Rear, famous NBA basketball player for the Philadelphia 76ers, had been charged with raping a team cheerleader. Dalton had phoned her for solace and courage. For Georgie, it had been a strange phone call, much like talking a man down from a skyscraper ledge.

And now with the recent announcement of Dalton's conversion to Islam and subsequent name change, Georgie cringed at the thought of a call from her old acquaintance. What kind of trouble could he be in now?

Was it true what the news magazines were insinuating? Had Ahmad written a letter threatening to assassinate the pro-nationalist President? Georgie didn't want to be in the news again, particularly for sympathizing with a fugitive from justice. She was still stinging from the East Side Riot exposure, her image as an assaulted female police officer had been plastered all over local and national media. They'd made her look weak and vulnerable. She figured it was a miracle that she'd been promoted to detective on her first attempt two years later.

She interrupted Betty's scolding. "Play Ahmad Elali's recording, please."

The older woman huffed a sigh and played the audio.

"I'm sorry I missed her," Ahmad had said. "Tell her I'll call again later."

The voice was indeed Ahmad's. Georgie couldn't deny that. But it didn't have the offensive sound bites that had brought him recent fame. It was a small weary sound like that of a man who had resigned himself to do something desperate. Georgie did her best to dismiss images of the man lying in a pool of blood at the foot of a skyscraper, his limbs spread in unnatural angles on the pavement.

"Chief Gray wants you and Miltie back in his office. ASAP," Betty said.

"We're still following up on some leads with the Bobby K. case."

"That'll keep," she said, taking a slurp of something. The woman was a caffeine addict. "Urgent meeting with Chief Gray."

"Okay, if you say so." Georgie paused, her mind circling back to Ahmad. "Did Ahmad leave a phone number, Betty?"

She gave Georgie a number with a DC prefix, and Georgie thanked her before signing off. Did the infamous Brother Ahmad live in the nation's capital now? Georgie couldn't remember. She prayed Ahmad was still alive, and she prayed the President was also.

Georgie zipped her leather jacket back up and braced herself against the cold before stepping out of the car.

Hayes was two doors down, talking to a neighbor. Jaquan Pack was nowhere in sight.

Too bad.

She would have wanted to talk with the kid some more. At seventeen, the kid needed something better than dodging cops to fill his days. She'd heard the community center down the street had reopened. Maybe she and Hayes could swing by the place to meet the new director on their way back into headquarters. It was always a good idea to know the neighborhood leaders.

As she started walking toward her partner, Georgie saw another black Jag driving toward her or was it the same Jag? Wary, she stopped and stared. The driver stopped the car. Despite the fog, he seemed to be looking right at her. She let her eyes slide over in Hayes' direction. He was knocking on another door, further away.

You're on your own, Georgie girl. Just you and God. Breathe. Take it slow.

The driver's door opened, and her heart pounded. Something about the way the man moved seemed familiar. His head and upper body came into view, and her hand slid like hot butter over the handle of her gun. Then her bottom lip went slack. "Dr. Fields?"

"Miss Turner?" Dr. So Fine Fields hadn't changed much. A few gray hairs speckled his close-cropped beard and tiny crow's feet creased the corners of his smiling eyes, but it only added to his attraction. "Goodness, it is you."

He was a slow jam song in motion, and the sway of his upper body was the melody. The swagger of his lower, the harmony. In a few long strides, he stood in front of her, extending a hand. She shook it, relishing the warmth.

Find a God-fearing man? Mama, I found him.

46

Had he just walked right back into her life? This *had* to be God's doing.

Good God A'mighty.

She shook herself from her trance. "You had my cop senses tingling when you stopped in the middle of the street like that, had me worried."

"Sorry about that." He thrilled her with a deep-throated chuckle. "I drove by a few minutes ago on my way to pick up a student. There was a glare on your windshield, and I couldn't tell if it was indeed you sitting behind the wheel. When I saw you getting out of the car just now... I had to stop. Um ... I heard you were with the Rocky Mount PD."

Had he been following her career?

A good sign, I think...

She nodded. "I was with RMPD for a little over five years. Moved on after my mother died."

"Sorry to hear that. About your mother, that is."

She dipped her chin, suddenly shy about sharing something so personal. "Thank you."

Why was she blushing?

"No problem, *Officer* Turner."

Georgie rammed her cold hands in her jean pockets and took a couple easy steps toward him. His smile was like sweet cream stirred into the best black coffee. "Please, call me Georgie."

"Only if you call me Shawn."

Her smile gave way to a giggle.

You're flirting, girl.

Before a second thought compelled her to do otherwise, she asked the fifty thousand dollar question. "What are you doing here on the East Side, Shawn?"

It felt weird saying his first name. Could he hear the giddiness she felt? How many times had she evoked that name in her mind over the years? She'd lost count, but one thing she knew, she always felt butterflies whenever Shawn Fields came to mind. Was this chance meeting a sign of something good? She fingered one of her business cards in her pocket. Would he think her too forward if she gave him her number?

Shawn pointed up the street as he walked around the front of the car. "On my way to work. I'm the new director of the community center a few blocks down. You know the place, I'll bet."

Oh really?

She bit back a satisfied smile. "Congrats. I heard they'd reopened. In fact, I was just thinking about dropping by to introduce myself to the new director."

His smile widened, dimpling one side of his jaw.

Georgie studied his face, his actions. Was he flirting with her? She hoped so. The breeze shifted and she caught a whiff of his cologne. Subtle yet strong.

Take it easy.

A small brown face, framed in pigtails, appeared in the rear passenger seat, putting the brakes on her fantasy. A milk mustache graced the tiny girl's upper lip. She pushed herself higher in her car seat and yelled through the closed window. "Good morning, Dec'tive Turner."

The young girl's almond eyes made her go cold. It was Jaquan's little girl. Georgie searched her memory for her name. What kind of future did a teenage kid have when he was trying to raise a child?

Pushing her opinions aside, Georgie put on a happy face. "Well, good mornin' to you, little Destiny. How are you today?"

"Fine," the loud three-year-old chirped, "Mr. Shawn bought me breakfus." She held up a cereal bar and pint carton of milk. "Now he be takin' me to school."

"That's great."

Little Destiny Park nodded and stuffed a chunk of food in her mouth.

"Well," Shawn said as he backpedaled, "I'd better get this little one to daycare and get ready for a staff meeting."

Georgie pushed the business card deeper into her pocket.

"It was great to see you. Drop by sometime."

"Sure thing." She stepped away from the car, and seemingly, stepped back into reality as the warmth she'd felt under his gaze was wicked away by the chilly air. She was a cop. She had a job to do. She was not getting paid to bat her eyelashes at Dr. So Fine. "It was nice bumping into you."

"Have a blessed day, Georgie."

"You too, Shawn."

Georgie stood alone and watched Shawn slip behind the wheel of his black Jag and drive away. "Goodbye, Dr. So Fine. Just walk on by."

The week scuttled by like an East Side stray. No further calls from her old friend turned social activist. No Dr. So Fine sightings. And no leads on finding Bobby K. Chief Gray was sure the twenty-something Korean kid was linked to a recent spate of break-ins, but Georgie had her doubts about that.

The weather had improved, and the mild winter nights made Georgie dream of summer walks with Shawn. They would stroll hand-in-hand through downtown, talking softly about the smells in the air— an enticing tangle of fresh-baked bread, fried fish, and Italian spices. Eventually, they would stop for a bite to eat at ...

Stop it, woman.

Her pretend walk with Shawn had taken her past her townhouse door. As she doubled back, she noticed the huddled form of a man sitting on the bottom step. The lean figure rose and ambled along the walk with the detachment of a housecat. Georgie wanted to run past him into her apartment, not out of fear for her life necessarily, but out of dread for what the man approaching her would bring.

The composure in her own voice surprised her as she greeted the young man. "Hello, Bobby K. How you been?"

Bobby K. didn't waste time on chit-chat. "I been fencing stuff for this dude. Old guy. Tall, like you. Like he coulda played in the NBA or something. Told me to call him Dalton."

Georgie's heart dropped and her brain went blank.

Bobby kept talking. "The thing is. I ain't heard from him in a few days. He told me if this happened to come to you and turn myself in. I think he dead, and I think somebody's trying to kill me too. Take me in."

He took a step toward her then stood with his arms and legs spread wide, waiting to be frisked.

Dumbfounded, Georgie managed to pat him down and lead him to her car. She knew she wouldn't be seeing her bed tonight. She sent Hayes a quick text: **Bringing in Bobby K. RN.** Then started the car. Even though Milton Burle Hayes was old school, Georgie knew he would understand her texting shorthand and meet her at the station. He always came through.

"So, Bobby, sounds like you've been busy since the last time I patted you down."

The last time he'd assumed the position for Georgie had been three months earlier after breaking up a fist fight in the alley behind his parent's restaurant, Kwan's Diner.

Bobby K., real name Sung-woo Kwan, attended some culinary school in South Korea. The young man was bigger than most Koreans Georgie knew, and between his temper and his size, Mrs. Kwan's baby boy had a bad habit of attracting trouble. Though Georgie supposed his choice of attire helped him fit in with the black and mixed-race youth he hung around.

She decided to tread softly with Bobby. Tenderize him, in Haye's vernacular, before having him make a formal statement. Georgie checked her reflection in the rearview mirror. Even in the dark interior of her car, she could see the crease across her forehead.

Try not to look like a police detective, Georgie girl.

Bobby drew a breath and blew it out slowly. "Tryna make the ends meet, Detective Turner. You know me. Gotta hustle. Heard you ran my boy Jaquan down tryna find me."

She nodded.

"Y'all gonna be lenient with me, right? Cause I didn't have to turn myself in or nothing. You feel me?"

"Yeah, sure."

There was something about the way Bobby was talking yet not talking that was getting on her nerves. She didn't just smell a rat, she smelled a million fleas and the coming of a plague. "This isn't the time to negotiate, Mr. Kwan. I'm just assessing the situation you're in."

He turned his face to the passenger side window.

Georgie persisted. "Somebody stalking you?"

Bobby K. shrugged and muttered something in Korean. She was able to pick out a couple cuss words.

"Okay, Bobby, let's pretend that I'm not a police detective. You're just sitting down with me in the back booth of your parent's restaurant, waiting for a bowl of kimchi stew. Let's pretend we're having a nice cozy conversation about your life."

"What?" He looked at her. Was that fear in his eyes? "I was nearly killed, lady. Somebody chased me last night. Shot at me. I been hiding out on this side of town all day waiting for you to come home. Let's just say I've followed you home a time or two. Okay?"

"You should consider working for law enforcement, Bobby. You got major surveillance skills."

He grunted and went on. "I'ma be honest with you, Turner. I ain't been this scared in my life. You know me. I do petty stuff, fencing mostly for the gangs. It's my way of staying out of their way. I help them, they don't mess with my family."

"Interesting logic."

"Don't judge me. My family is all I got." His shoulders sank. He looked at his hands in his lap. "Anyway, I don't own no gun. Ain't never hurt nobody. 'Cept in a fist fight, I guess. But nothing deadly. This Dalton dude looked me up a few weeks ago. Said he wanted me to sell some big-ticket items for him. He needed lots of money, real fast. I moved tons of high-end TVs, diamonds, iPhones for him. Real quick. I turned over five grand for him and I guess he thought he could trust me. Invited me to his place."

"*His* place?"

Did Bobby K. really know where Dalton aka Ahmad lived? This was unreal.

"Yeah, turns out, he lives in this duplex on Fenton."

"In Chow Town?"

He nodded. "I went over there and we ended up getting drunk together, even smoked a little weed. He got to talking about this plan to shake mess up big time in this country. I couldn't make much sense of it all 'cause he was so drunk and high. He just needed money to bankroll his plan, you know. Skip the country for a long time. Something about a letter to the President."

Georgie pulled into her parking spot at the station and killed the engine. She tried to hide her surprise. "You'd better not be pulling my leg, Bobby."

He held his hands up in surrender. "I ain't lying, Turner. This dude was in some big trouble. The mob or somebody was after him, I think. That's why he was laying low in Chow Town, building up his cash flow so he could leave the country for a while. That's what he told me."

Georgie's cell phone vibrated as she got out of the car. It was a text from Hayes. **Right behind you.**

A pair of headlights swept across the parking lot. She recognized Hayes' '82 Buick as she walked Bobby to the police station.

Bobby became more animated. "Promise me you'll protect my family. Whoever was after Dalton knows who I am. That's who was after me last night. They probably know how to get at my family."

Hayes sauntered up. "Evening. Look who we got here, Turner."

"Evening, Miltie," Georgie said, using Hayes' nickname. "Turned himself in. Says he's got something on Brother Ahmad."

"Wait a minute," Bobby said. "Dalton won't his real name? I knew something won't right. When he was drunk, he kept talking about some dude called Brother Ekeme. I heard that name in the news. Some militant black group against the President."

Hayes shot Georgie a glance as he reached around Bobby to open the station door. "That would be Louis Ekeme, famed leader of the black nationalists group called The Brotherhood. Come with me, Bobby K. We'll have a little talk. Just you and me and a little recorder."

Georgie stood alone in the parking lot for a few minutes. Her heart was heavy with a crazy mixture of anger and concern for Ahmad and Bobby K., but she let her mind travel back to her street where she still strolled with Shawn. Fingers entwined. Longing for intimacy.

She turned her face heavenward and inhaled the mild January breeze. "Help me know your will for my life, dear Lord."

"Ya done good, Georgie!" Hayes said and flashed her a rare smile.

"Thanks, partner." She rubbed her sleepy eyes and leaned back in her desk chair. "Truth be told, the good Lord laid that one right in my lap. You did your part too. Well done."

She gave him back the report he'd written containing Bobby K.'s account. Too weary to think straight, she'd only scanned it but knew that Hayes had dotted every *i* and crossed every single *t*. That was just his way.

Now all they had to do was follow up on Bobby's leads and find Ahmad. Easy peasy. Case closed.

She and Hayes made a great team. What would she do without him when he retired in a few years? Their little celebration was short-lived. Chief Gray waddled by on the way to his office and gave Georgie a nod. He pointed to his office and mumbled something about wanting to see both of them in five minutes.

Hayes's voice dropped to a whisper. "Rumor has it, Wonder Woman, that you're gonna be reassigned. Put on TDY with the FBI coming to bring Ahmad Elali and maybe Louis Ekeme in."

Georgie stifled a yawn. "Don't listen to rumor."

Hayes followed her as they navigated through a bunch of donut-eating uniforms to Chief Gray's office.

Georgie spoke over her shoulder to him. "I've been thinking about quitting, Miltie... after you retire, that is."

Hayes dismissed her with a wave. "Stuff and nonsense, woman."

They nodded at Betty and invited themselves into Gray's office.

Chief Thelonius Gray gathered his suit coat across his broad middle and stood. "Great work, you two."

Hayes took a seat. "It was Georgie's doing." Fearful of nodding off, Georgie stood by the door.

She watched Chief Gray wander to his window where he studied the Raleigh skyline backlit by the rosy hues of early morning.

"If you have to start your day before the crack of dawn, it's nice to have a little good news," he said before turning to face them. Launching into his monotone mode, he explained, without any frills, what would happen to Bobby K. and the Kwan family.

"We're bringing in a couple FBI agents," Gray relayed.

"Told ya," Hayes whispered to Georgie.

Georgie gave a deeper frown. *Federal fuzz.*

"Okay, Georgie," Chief Gray continued, "I know you grew up with Ahmad, but he's as dirty as I am fat and black. He's bad news. We all know that." He returned to his desk and shuffled some files around, then handed folders to Hayes and Georgie. "What you have there is everything the Feds have shared with us on Ahmad and his newfound religious organization, The Brotherhood. We already have a unit headed to the Chow Town address Bobby Kwan gave us. Georgie, I want you there ASAP."

"There, sir?"

"In Chow Town. You'll be relocated to the police surveillance apartment on the East Side. 564 Fenton."

Hayes gave a dry chuckle. "Chow Town."

In shock, Georgie said nothing.

As she shaved her legs in her new shower, Georgie's mind created the shapes, sounds, and smells of another person in the bathroom with her. Her hips would brush his thigh as he leaned closer to the mirror to apply shaving cream. He'd do that face-stretching thing that men always do when they shave. He'd lean back and give her a sweet little peck on her lips. She'd give him a love pat on the rear. Later, they'd share the morning paper over bowls of oatmeal and eggs. That's what married couples did, right? And before they parted ways for the day, he'd wrap his delightfully-scented body around her while asking God's blessings on their workday.

Georgie turned off the razor and sighed. "Oh, Shawn."

This loneliness weighed heavier on her than ever before. Meeting Shawn in the street several days ago had been wreaking havoc with her mind. Being in the same neighborhood only made it worse.

No. What made it worse was knowing her life was not her own. She was almost thirty-five and still married to the job. The force told her what she could and could not do. The police force was her master. And a jealous master, at that. He didn't allow room for a real-life husband and kids.

She'd been in Chow Town, entombed in her new digs on Fenton Street, for a full twenty-four hours. In her ten years in law enforcement, Georgie had been on her share of stakeouts, but this was different. This was ten times worse. On a normal surveillance job, she was with a partner. That other person helped you pass the time with a chummy card game, helped you stay alert, kept you from losing every single one of your marbles.

After finishing her shower and getting dressed, she went back into the kitchen for breakfast...and to watch the CCTV monitors. There were five of them. Five big eyes on the free world. Five quiet companions. For how long, though? Nobody knew.

Under the cover of darkness, officers armed with a search warrant had entered the address Bobby K. had identified, two doors down. Instead of finding Ahmad, they'd only found traces that he'd been there. From the mail clogging his box, he'd been gone for several days. While she returned to her townhouse to pack a couple of bags, her boss had arranged for discreet high-tech cameras to be installed in and around Ahmad's place. In the first day of surveillance, she'd observed absolutely nothing via the cameras or from her line of sight. Not even a stray cat.

It was for the best, she imagined. Staying in Chow Town would have been harder if she had been required to beat the pavement every day for hours on end. At least this way, none of the East Side residents knew she was here and she didn't have to smell the stench from the dog food factory just across Walnut Creek. Best of all, she didn't have to relive the attack from the riots five years earlier. She was safe here, relatively speaking. Agents were embedded elsewhere in the neighborhood, watching the same house from a different angle at night while she slept.

In the big scheme, she wasn't alone in this operation. So, why did she feel lonely?

Georgie carried her bowl of Cheerios to the kitchen window. She watched a pair of teenage boys amble by, their pants hanging low. Traffic was surprisingly heavy for this time of day, so she counted the school buses. The taxi cabs. The hoopties. All while keeping an eye on the monitors. *It's going to be another long day*, she told herself.

A black Jaguar sedan pulled into the double driveway of her duplex, and Georgie's eyes sprang open. She put her bowl in the sink and strained to see the driver exiting the car. All she could see was the tail end of the car, but she could hear the driver talking to someone.

"Hello, Vanessa, I just got in from the airport."

The dark-chocolate voice of the man speaking was extremely familiar.

Shawn Fields.

She held her breath and scurried toward the front door where she hoped to catch a glimpse of him as he approached the other door of the duplex. A shadow fell across the porch, showing an outline of a tall man with something, most likely a cell phone, held to his ear. Georgie stepped back a bit so as not to reveal her presence to him.

Shawn kept talking as keys rattled. "I'm going to take a quick shower and change clothes, but I should be in for staff meeting by eight this morning. Thank you for picking up Destiny and holding down the fort the past couple days. You are the best assistant ever. See you later."

Georgie couldn't believe her ears. Shawn Fields lived on the other side of the duplex. Dr. So Fine lived in Chow Town. There was a God. Even though she couldn't let him know she was there, it still felt good to be near him. Things were looking up.

The day couldn't go by fast enough for Georgie. The good doctor returned at dusk. Minutes after returning home, he changed into workout clothes and left for a jog. Of course, she watched his every move as far as she could see down Fenton before he ran across the bridge that led to the Purina plant.

Her cell phone alarm went off, signaling the end of her workday. She phoned her Federal counterparts to verify the handoff of surveillance. After logging a quick but concise report for the day, she entertained thoughts of a jog herself... over the river and through the way.

Sudden pounding on Shawn's door caused her to abort that thought. Georgie pressed herself against the living room wall and listened.

"Mr. Shawn! Mr. Shawn!"

It was Jaquan. No doubt about it, but what was he doing at Shawn's door?

"I found Dalton," Jaquan said in a loud whisper. "I think he hurt. I need your help." Another series of bangs on the door. "Yo! You in there?"

After waiting for several more seconds, Jaquan jumped off the porch and trotted to a bicycle lying in the driveway. He rode away at a fast pace while glancing back twice. She watched him until he also rode across the bridge heading toward the plant.

Something was definitely fishy. How badly was Dalton hurt? What was the connection between Jaquan, Dalton, and Shawn? She didn't know quite what was going on, but she was going to get to the bottom of it, on duty or not. After grabbing her car keys, her phone, and her gun, she phoned in, requesting backup at the plant.

By the time she located her car one block over and crossed the bridge, neither Jaquan nor Shawn were anywhere in sight. Georgie spotted an abandoned red and blue bicycle beside one of the many rusted-out warehouses. Had Jaquan's bicycle been red and blue? She couldn't remember but stopped anyway. She called in her position and killed her engine. A nearby streetlight provided some illumination.

Using her cell phone light, she scanned the area. There were tire tracks in the gravel parking lot that looked as fresh as her tire marks. Was someone still in the building? She glanced at her phone, it was after 6 p.m. She had called for backup more than five minutes ago. What was taking so long?

She took a deep breath and released it slowly. No use waiting.

Lord, I pray for your protection and guidance.

She donned her Kevlar vest and left the car, gun at the ready. The sound of her footsteps across the damp gravel seemed overly loud in the early evening stillness.

Then she heard talking.

She pressed her back against the side of the warehouse and strained to distinguish the words.

"Dalton?" someone yelled. "You okay, man? I got a friend with me. His name Shawn."

It was Jaquan's voice, but she couldn't make out the response. On tiptoe, she eased sideways through the door and slipped inside. A little light from outside filtered into the warehouse. She made out two people, one much larger than the other, standing near a door at the far end, some thirty feet away. Several stacks of boxes and barrels separated her from them.

Georgie crept along the outside wall, careful to place a barrier between her and the others. Was this a trap? Better safe than sorry. She'd stay hidden a while longer.

She ducked behind a wooden crate and checked her firearm. It was good to go. Someone rattled a doorknob. Was Jaquan moving in?

"Can you open the door from your side?" That was Shawn's voice.

There was a muffled response from the other side of the door. She inched forward.

Somehow Jaquan had caught up with Shawn on the road over, but why were they working together to begin with? If that was indeed Brother Ahmad locked behind the door, why wasn't he able to get out? Who put him there and why?

Georgie worked her way slowly through the maze of dusty boxes to within ten feet of the pair. "Hold it right there," she yelled. "This is the police."

Jaquan and Shawn spun around in shock.

"Hands up. Fingers laced over your heads," she barked.

Though visibly confused, they obeyed.

"Georgie?" Shawn asked. "What's going on?"

"I should be asking you two the same thing." She stepped into a patch of light and pointed her gun at Shawn. "Who is in there?"

"A man named Dalton," Shawn said. "One of Jaquan's friends. We think he's hurt, but the door is either locked or blocked. We hear noise inside like someone is trying to talk to us. I think he's bound and can't—"

"Two steps to the left please," Georgie commanded. "Then turn to face the wall and drop down on your knees."

They both did as she said.

"We've done nothing wrong," Shawn said.

"Yeah, Detective Turner," Jaquan added. "We ain't done nothing bad. Dalton been paying me to run packages 'round the city for him for a few months. Gotta do something to put food in my baby's mouth. Shawn been taking my little girl to school, he been nothing but good to me. I figured he'd be able to get Dalton to the hospital, but the door is locked."

Well, that explained their connection at least. Now to solve the mystery behind Door Number One. She approached the door and turned the knob. Locked.

"Hello," she spoke to whoever was inside, "this is Detective Turner. Can you hear me?"

A muffled response.

She looked around for something heavy. "We need to open the door."

"We can help you, Georgie," Shawn assured. "I ... we would never hurt you. You can trust us."

She could barely make out his features in the dim interior, but his words held sincerity. She took out her phone. 6:13pm and no backup.

Jaquan spoke up. "We need to get him out before they come back."

She turned on her cell phone flashlight and scanned the area. Her beam fell across what looked like a metal sheet a few feet away. Hopefully, it wasn't too heavy to use as a battering ram. "They? Who's they?"

"The dudes what locked Dalton in there. I seen a car circling 'round his place for a day or two. Started seeing it after y'all took Bobby K. in. Where y'all took him anyway?"

That had been federal agents, she figured, but she wasn't going to tell him that. Just like she wasn't about to let them know that city and federal forces had been watching over the neighborhood for quite a while because there was always trouble in Chow Town.

"Never mind Bobby K. ..." Georgie started, but an explosion of gunfire from the entrance cut her short.

"Get down," she yelled, diving for the nearest crate.

A wail of police sirens filled the air.

Finally.

Jaquan dashed past her and lunged for the sheet of metal. Gunfire followed his path, ricocheting off the sheet as he lifted it. A second later, sharp pain peppered her right upper arm. She screamed.

I'm hit.

She managed to return a couple rounds before crumpling to her knees behind some boxes. The pain took her breath away. She squeezed her eyes tight and grit her teeth. The darkness became darker.

Focus. Focus. C'mon, Georgie. Focus.

Someone pulled her to the ground and covered her with their body. Her mind swam sluggishly. Sounds were muddied with flashing red and blue lights. The lights had sounds? Men were shouting. More gunfire. In the midst of the chaos, the sweet musky scent of a man's cologne lingered near.

The sensation of cool fingers on her forehead brought Georgie around. She opened her eyes. Shawn was smiling down at her. Beeping hospital monitors surrounded them. She felt loopy and lightheaded, but the pain was gone. She looked down and studied the white bandage hugging her right shoulder and bicep.

"Hello, Miss Turner," Shawn said.

"Hello, Dr. So Fine." She giggled and clasped a hand over her mouth.

He chuckled. "What was that?"

"I can't believe I said that out loud."

Shawn laughed again. "Me either. That one took me back to my Central days for real. I heard about the names and little ditties you ladies had for me."

"Oh, really?"

"Good thing I was too focused on getting tenure. Could have scared a brother off."

They laughed together.

"I'm glad you're awake," he said. "You've been out for about twelve hours. Hayes said your brother is flying in."

"Hayes?"

"He's getting a cup of coffee. He'll be back soon. Says he feels bad that he wasn't there for you. You two go way back, I guess?"

Georgie nodded. "We've been together since I made detective. But I've known him since the East Side Riot. We spend a lot of time on the East Side. There's always trouble in Chow Town."

"Not always." Shawn frowned and looked like he was going to say something but shook his head and nodded toward her wound. "They got Dalton out of that room. He'd been gagged and bound for days so he was dehydrated. He's here in the hospital too but under armed guard. Federal agents are trying to find the men who did that to him."

"I'm glad he's alive. He's in big trouble though."

Shawn agreed with a nod, still studying her arm. "I'm sorry about your arm."

"Thanks for being here." She looked him in the eye. "And thanks for protecting me. You didn't get hit?"

Shawn shook his head. "That was God's grace and mercy. When you got hit ... it didn't matter if I got shot too. I had to protect you."

She blinked. "You been getting some of these happy drugs too?"

He smiled. "I've always been sweet on you, Georgetta May Turner. While I was climbing the tenure ladder, I watched you from afar. Overcoming financial difficulties. Becoming an accomplished student leader on that campus. You're a force to be reckoned with, for sure."

She blushed.

He went on. "But you love God and you love justice. I saw you bring the brightest lights out of the roughest areas surrounding Central's campus. One of the teens you used to mentor is a medical doctor now. Another works in criminal justice like you."

Tears stung her eyes. She had no idea. She was so focused on her own career that she'd never looked back.

Shawn cradled her free hand in his. "With God's guidance ... and a little help from me ...maybe you can see Chow Town differently. Maybe you can see me differently. I'm more than a pretty face and ... I'll never walk by you again."

Never again, Dr. So Fine.

"Is this where you kiss me?"

He gave her a lopsided grin and leaned closer. "I thought you'd never ask."

About the Author

Linda Leigh Hargrove has been designing for web and print media for more than fifteen years. She's an engineer, a multi-published fiction author, a mother of three boys, and a wife of more than twenty-five years. Linda is a North Carolina native and tinkers on 3D printers in her free time. Her life motto, "She is no fool who gives what she cannot keep to gain what she cannot lose", governs every writing decision. Find out more about her work at LLHargrove.com.

Love Walked In

Love Won't Let Me Wait
Patricia A. Bridewell

Chapter 1

"Stop, stop!" Sister Lorraine said, waving her hands. "Okay, y'all. Some folks are hitting flat notes. Don't act like you never sang acapella before. We want our new pianist to walk into harmony. Now, sing from your soul." She swung her arms back and forth. "One and two and three." The choir started singing.

Jamila Parker glanced over the Mount Everest Church of Christ choir before she cracked a smile so hard it made her face hurt. *This rehearsal really sucks.* Never had they sounded so lackluster in all the years she'd been singing with them.

Yes, most of the choir spoke out about Dale's resignation after seven years of service as minister of music. It didn't make sense. Why would he leave after achieving two Best Choir of the Year Awards and one Stellar Award under his leadership? And right before their live recording session for Charity Record Company.

Within minutes, Sister Lorraine's encouragement evoked new life in the forty-two member choir. Jamila's soprano voice was right on key until...a Godiva Chocolate, Chadwick Boseman-looking brother entered and trekked down the middle aisle. In a daze, her eyes stayed fixed on him. She finally realized she'd stopped singing and made a quick recovery. *Mercy! That can't be the piano player.*

Dressed in a black suit and gray shirt unbuttoned to mid-chest, topped with a gray hat, he possessed a swagger and confidence that sent Jamila's mind spinning. *Breathtaking!* She pressed a hand against her chest to calm a runaway heartbeat.

A nudge in the side distracted her attention from the man. "What?" Jamila whispered, frowning at her friend, Chanelle.

"You know," Chanelle whispered, attempting not to laugh.

Standing in the front row, Jamila was privy to the fragrance of the handsome brother's cologne when he walked by. *Lord, please forgive me.* After he approached the piano, he turned and surveyed the choir. His eyes stalled on Jamila, a smile as big as the moon stretched from ear-to-ear. Jamila returned the smile and diverted her attention.

A deep voice brought her back to the present. "Let's talk after rehearsal," Otis whispered over her shoulder. Jamila hadn't noticed that he'd crept in late and taken a seat behind hers. She cut her eyes at Otis and leaned into his ear. "No." *Why did he decide to move back to L.A.?* Otis twisted his mouth and shot a glare at the piano player.

The song ended, and so did the engaging moment with Mr. Dreamboat. Otis had ruined a potential opportunity to explore a new friendship. She was tired of hearing his same old broke down story about rekindling their relationship. She was over him.

Jamila sensed Sister Lorraine's annoyance with their whispering by the frown that never faded. They had three weeks to prepare for the recording, and it would be interesting to see how Dale's replacement and Sister Lorraine coordinated the project.

"Okay, ladies and gentlemen, he's here. This is Brother Nolan Spencer." Sister Lorraine turned to Mr. Dreamboat. "Brother Nolan, please tell us a little about yourself."

Mr. Dreamy stood and did a partial bow. "Thank you, Sister Lorraine. Uh, first, my apologies for arriving late." He rubbed his goatee. "I got tripped up in that crazy L.A. traffic."

The choir broke out in laughter, Jamila smiled and crossed her legs.

"I'm originally from Indiana. However, I've been around, traveled, and lived in various places. God blessed me with this job, and I'm grateful to work with all of you."

"Is your family here?" One of the female choir members asked with a grin.

"No, I'm here alone." Nolan stole a quick glance at Jamila and buttoned his jacket. "Been playing since I was nine and writing gospel music for twenty-two of my thirty-five years on earth. Praise God."

"Amens" echoed in the choir stand.

He pointed at the choir, "Man, all I can say is... Wow, you all can *sang*. I'll turn it back over to Sister Lorraine."

"Amen," Sister Lorraine said. "Thank you, Brother Nolan. Come on y'all, let's give our new pianist *and* minister of music a round of applause. He's part of our team."

Minister of Music? He can get my clap anytime. Jamila jumped up and applauded before giving Chanelle, who was still seated, the side eye. *What's on her mind?* Chanelle checked her watch, squirmed to the edge of her seat and then stood.

"Time to get down to business." Sister Lorraine stroked her short cut. "Y'all know we don't have much time left. Right? So, drop your personal business outside and focus on singin'. Did I make myself clear?"

Chanelle and Jamila glanced at one another, then nodded their heads. Jamila turned and squinted at Otis, wishing she could scrape that blank stare off his face. She owed him nothing, and the gall to approach her during choir rehearsal was inappropriate. *Unbelievable.* Jamila would not give him another opportunity to make a fool out of her. Once, twice, then five times of cheating and lying was the max. And a relationship with another woman who had his baby was the end of Mr. Casanova's reign over her life.

"Okay, let's break for fifteen minutes. After that, we'll rehearse another forty-five minutes with the entire choir, then y'all can leave. Except Destiny's Peace." Sister Lorraine adjusted her red-framed glasses that had slipped down her nose. "You'll rehearse another forty-five minutes with Brother Nolan."

Chanelle sighed. Jamila noticed the scowl on her friend's ebony brown face. She couldn't blame Chanelle for being upset. The woman had a husband and three kids at home, plus she was in school. "Hey, sister girl, you wanna chat?"

"Why not?" Chanelle snatched her jacket from the seat. "I can't go home, and Darius will be upset. I can't be rehearsing late like this."

"I hear you, but Darius should be used to this." Jamila watched Sister Lorraine and Nolan conversing. *There goes my plan to personally welcome Mr. Dreamy to the Mount Everest family during break.*

"Girl, come on," Chanelle told Jamila. "Fifteen minutes will end before we reach the door."

They entered the lobby, and Otis blocked Jamila's path. "I've been calling you for weeks. Can I get a minute with you?" His soulless eyes stared in her face. No hello or how are you, just a cold expression.

"Uh, I don't have time." She stepped around him as two choir members walked past, whispering on their way out.

"Go on and talk. I need to check in with Darius." Chanelle went speed walking through the exit.

Jamila was trapped. Darn it, Chanelle! You were supposed to have my back. You know I don't want to be left alone with this man. "Five minutes and I mean it."

Otis rolled his shoulders. "All right."

The winter chill grazed her jaws when she pushed the door open. She stuffed her arms in a black trench coat and tossed a wrap around her neck as they dashed to her Honda Accord. After she got in the car, she turned on the heat and rubbed her hands together. Otis sat in silence sulking. That raised red flags that made her uneasy.

"Why are you sitting there? Talk or I'm going back inside."

"I don't get you. I came back here confident we'd get back together." Otis cast his gaze out the window. "You haven't forgiven me. I was straight with you when that DNA test came back about my baby. The worst day of my life and you threw me over a cliff. That hurt me."

Jamila sighed. "Worst day of your life? Don't even go there. Between your side pieces and bad temper, then you knock some woman up, too?" She shook her head. "Talk about hurt. Trust me, you don't know what real hurt is. I've moved on."

"Yeah, I bet you have. I saw you eyeing the new *minister of music.* You got the hots for him already?"

"Look, I don't know that man. Besides, that's none of your business."

"Oh, it's my business. I'm not going away. I love you." He put his arm around her shoulder and pushed his face against hers. She pushed him away.

"Get off me. I shouldn't have come out here." On edge about his behavior, she unlocked the car and hopped out. "And stop leaving messages on my cell."

"Babe, come on. Give me another chance," Otis begged in a whiny child-like voice, climbing out of the passenger side. She hit the alarm and sprinted back toward the building.

"I'm not letting you go," he shouted, running after her. Jamila was grateful no one else was around or that could've stirred up old chaos and gossip in the church.

"Otis, why don't you stop? Do I need to call security?" Chanelle said, catching up with Jamila. She touched Jamila's arm. "You okay?"

Jamila shook her head. "Girl, don't ever leave me with him. He's got a problem."

Otis had claimed he was the 'right guy' and would put a ring on her finger. But, she was done with that lying cheater. Because of him, she'd almost been kicked out of the choir, the Destiny's Peace group, and the church. After they broke up a year ago, he had one of his angry tantrums, and lied saying she'd slept with other men in the church. Jamila almost walked away from Mount Everest on her own, and then Bishop Evans asked Otis to take a leave from the church to get his head together. Right guy, alright...

He was as right as an athlete wearing stilettos to run a track meet.

Chapter 2

Jamila tried to avoid resting her eyes on Nolan, but that was impossible. While the six members of Destiny's Peace rehearsed, he played. And did he ever play — like a musical genius playing at a stadium concert.

He made it his business to glance at Jamila often. Although flattering, she felt he should keep his wandering eyes under control.

The song ended with a flourish. "Hallelujah!" He clapped, "You all sounded fabulous. Okay, Jamila, Sister Lorraine told me you're leading *Walk by Faith,* right?"

"Yes, I'm ready," Jamila removed the microphone from the stand.

Nolan lifted a hand to cue and started playing. Jamila began singing, and he sprung up, playing on his feet throughout the whole song. Happiness over his reaction transitioned into a question. *Why would a handsome young man with so much talent not be married? He said he was here alone, but he might have a wife sitting at home.*

Discouraged, Jamila was tired of dating. At thirty-one, she'd accepted that she may never find true love. Three wasted years and a breakup with Otis almost broke her spirit before she turned it over to God.

Nolan lifted another hand to close the song. "Awesome! That's a wrap for tonight. Did Sister Lorraine tell you we'll need to bump rehearsal up to two evenings?"

"Two evenings a week?" Chanelle asked. The group looked baffled.

"Nah, she didn't mention that," one of the group members said. The others agreed.

He crossed one leg over the other and smiled. "Now hear me out, I just got to L.A. But, it's like this. You're talented, but to get that recording contract, you must strive for creative growth. An audition with Charity Record Company don't get any better. I'll bring in the other musicians this week."

"Which days are we rehearsing?" Chanelle asked.

"Sister Lorraine will touch bases tomorrow. Enjoy your evening. Oh, Sister Jamila," Nolan gestured with an index finger, "can I holla at you before you leave?"

"Okay." Jamila felt a little embarrassed walking over to the piano.

Chanelle hugged her. "Talk to you tomorrow. I'm outta here."

"Sister Jamila, I've gotta say that soprano voice of yours is golden." He held up his hands in defense. "I'm not trying to sweet talk or get at you, but, Lady, where did you learn to sing like that?"

Jamila smiled. "Music is my passion. I majored in Music at Stanford."

He leaned back and nodded his head. "Whoa! A professionally trained singer, now that's not common in this business."

"Hmm...I wouldn't say *all* my training came from Stanford. But I learned a lot while I was there. I've been singing since I was in the first grade."

"I understand you write too. Is *Walk by Faith* your song?"

She tilted her head. "It is, and I have many more."

"Cool, I'd love to talk with you about your songs." He rolled his wrist and checked the time. "I know it's kinda late. You want to have dinner or grab a cup of coffee? I'm sure the cleaning crew will be rolling through here any minute now."

Jamila pushed her sandy-red hair from her face and shook her head. "I don't think so, I'm kind of tired this evening."

Nolan stared at her. "You'll have to excuse me for staring at you. Your red-bone skin and hair is beautiful."

"You like my hair? It's not dyed or a weave." She laughed and fluffed her kinky-curly mane. "I got teased so much when I was younger."

He shrugged. "Well, it didn't hurt to ask, and yes, "I do like it."

"Right. Tell you what. Take my number and call me," she smiled.

"Absolutely." He removed his phone from his jacket. "Shoot with the digits."

"It's 323-563-8892."

He tapped Jamila's number in his phone and called her. After she saved his number, she focused on Nolan, who was packing sheet music in a Samsonite briefcase. Long fingers with short manicured nails and clear polish meant he cared about his appearance. She liked that.

What am I doing? This gorgeous man just asked me out and I said 'no'. When the church sisters find out that he's the new minister of music, he'll have tons of digits by the end of Sunday services. This may be my only chance.

Jamila studied Nolan. "Please don't judge me. I don't know why I said 'no'. Can we still go eat?"

A slow smile crossed Nolan's face. "Sure thing. You'll have to decide where, and I'll follow you."

"Denny's," Jamila said.

"Denny's? Are you serious?"

"It's close by. I think it's too late to go anywhere else."

"Cool."

As soon as they walked out the door, she recognized Otis's cherry red Honda Jeep parked on the street. *What does he want now?* She wanted to escape to her car without any more drama.

Nolan frowned. "Something wrong?"

"Yes, let's go to our cars. I'll explain later."

They walked briskly to the parking lot, stopping at Jamila's car first. While giving Nolan the address to Denny's, she heard the roar of a car engine. Her eyes widened, and she screamed as Otis raced through the parking lot, circling her car multiple times.

Nolan jumped in front of Jamila, shielding her from danger. "What's he doing?" The brakes screeched and Otis stopped. Within seconds, he circled her car several more times before he stopped again in front of her car with high beams on. Otis started honking the horn nonstop.

"We should leave, now." Jamila said.

Nolan shook his head. "Hold on. Who's that dude?"

"My ex. We broke up a year ago. Go to your car, I don't want any problems."

"I'm not doing that. He don't scare me." Nolan held his ground and spread his arms out with splayed fingers. "What's up man? Get out the car," he flared his nostrils. Several minutes passed, and when Otis didn't budge, Nolan started toward him.

"No, don't do that," Jamila grabbed his arm. "He's not worth the fight, and you're new here."

"If you say so. I was gonna tell that brother something he would never forget. He could've hurt us driving that fast. I need to alert Bishop Evans immediately."

Otis gunned his engine and sped out of the lot. *Now, that was crazy.* Nolan was right. Bishop Evans would have to be notified to avoid another dangerous situation.

Chapter 3

Jamila's cell chimed playing *Victory Belongs to Jesus* by Todd Dulaney. This song had provided spiritual nourishment for the past year, and she woke up to it every morning. There was nothing more therapeutic than starting her day with prayer and music. She turned on her side and glanced at the clock and then her cell.

The time she spent with Nolan last night kept replaying in her head. She found his charisma enchanting, and he'd made her smile. The way he loved music and God was powerful. They didn't stay long at Denny's, but Jamila wanted to know more about him. For the moment, she'd settle for lying in bed thinking sweet thoughts about him. The phone stopped, and a minute later it started chiming again.

"Now who is this?" Jamila rubbed her eyes and picked up the phone. She checked the screen and answered. "Sister Girl, what you want this early?"

"Spit it out and don't hold back nothin', I gotta fix breakfast in a bit," Chanelle said.

Jamila laughed. "Breakfast? On a Saturday? Girl, Deon is nine. You better teach that boy how to fix some Frosted Flakes on the weekend. That'll leave you and Darius some snuggle-up time."

"Ple-e-a-se. Snuggle-up time is rare with three kids at home. Now forget about me and start talkin'."

"Nothing happened."

"Uh, huh. That man's eyes stayed on you. Don't play me. Did he hit on you?"

"Kind of, but Otis almost screwed up our night. I believe he has lost his mind. He tried to scare us, racing all through the parking lot."

"That's crazy. I hope you called the police."

Jamila yawned. "Nope. He didn't get far with the scare tactics. Nolan was ready to box, and he wasn't playing. Otis left, we went to Denny's." Chanelle had her own problems and telling her all her business probably wasn't the best idea. But they'd had each other's backs since high school, and her bestie was one of the few people she confided in. Except Grandma Ruth, her paternal grandmother. And she'd passed away.

"It's time to ask Celeste about filing that restraining order. Now, back to Nolan. He couldn't do better than Denny's?"

"You know me. I don't hang a huge dinner bill on my first dates. I mean he's new to L.A., and his funds might be tight." Jamila sat up and retied her silk scarf. "Denny's was my suggestion, and we didn't stay long. But we're going out again tonight."

Chanelle laughed. "I knew he was attracted to you. Don't mess this one up."

"Mess what up?"

"What I mean is give him a break. Also, find out who you're dating to avoid surprises. You've gotta stop falling for the jerks like Otis. And Tony with the three baby mamas. You deserve better."

Loser Tony. Erased from my mind as though he'd never existed. "Are you through bashing my love life?"

"What love life? I'm keeping you in check."

"I know. Girl, bye. I need some more rest." Jamila would never admit it, but Chanelle was right. She wasn't an expert when it came to choosing men.

Asking for her sister's help would result in a repetition of her mother's words. Celeste and Mama didn't care for Otis from the time they met him, and they had obviously picked up on character traits Jamila missed. The last thing she wanted was another 'I told you so' related to Otis.

Jamila propped pillows behind her back and scrolled Facebook, searching for a profile on Nolan Spencer. Nothing on Facebook, Twitter, or Instagram. *All of his accomplishments in the entertainment business and he doesn't have a social media profile?*

There was a knock on her bedroom door.

"Come in."

"How's life?" Her sister Celeste asked, sitting at the foot of the bed.

"I'm worn out. We rehearsed a long time last night."

"I don't know where you find time to write songs, sing, and work. Mama said the choir is recording soon. You didn't tell me."

"CeCe, with your schedule and mine, when do we cross paths?" Jamila massaged the tension in her neck, checking texts. "Charity Record Company signed the choir three weeks ago. My group is auditioning for a contract."

"Sounds fantastic," Celeste gave her two thumbs up. "If Destiny's Peace gets an offer, let me know. Your personal lawyer should review the contract before you sign. Philip has a friend who does entertainment law and he could handle the group if they're interested."

"I'll ask them."

"I'm leaving for the gym. You want to work out?"

"Not today, I'm resting for my date tonight." She scrolled through her text messages.

"A date? Who's this new guy?" Celeste placed a fist on her hip.

"It's not Otis. He's a renowned gospel singer and our new minister of music."

"Jami, that's great. I'm glad you're dating again." Celeste stretched and stood. "Hmm...an entertainer. I heard Otis is stalking you. When did he get back in town?"

Jamila raised her head, "I'm not sure if he ever left, but I told him to stop. I don't have time for his madness."

"Well, stalkers don't typically back off." Celeste rubbed her hands together. "We should talk about a restraining order."

"I'll do that. Not this week, though."

"*This* weekend. That's a priority, and I can file the restraining order on Monday. I'm heading out."

"I'll text you." After Celeste left, Jamila tossed her phone on the bed and picked up a pen and tablet from the nightstand, scribbling out words for her next song, *Tearless Love. Who told CeCe about my problems with Otis? Nothing is private at Mount Everest, people are always prying into other folks' business. I wish I could build a brick wall around my life and write songs day and night.* Jamila huffed and fell back against the bed.

Making the announcement about Nolan was a slip of the tongue. She had no intention of informing anybody but Chanelle about him, especially not her mother and CeCe. Wrong decisions encompassed a major part of her life. If a relationship with Nolan turned out to be a friendship, she wouldn't have to account for another one.

Chapter 4

The doorbell rang. Jamila panicked like a sixteen-year-old waiting for a prom date. She'd changed outfits five times before settling on a slinky off-the-shoulder black dress and dangling gold earrings. She dashed to the door but paused briefly to examine her appearance in a large hallway mirror. *Hair, makeup — in place. I'm ready.*

Nolan walked in holding a red rose; he kissed her cheek and handed it to her. He did a catcall whistle. "My, my, my, Lady, you smell so good, and your beauty is mind-blowing."

Jamila grinned. "Aww, you're so sweet. Have a seat while I put this rose in a vase." *Fabulous.*

Wow...nice crib," he glanced around the living room. "A fireplace too? May I ask what you do for a living?"

"I'm an administrative assistant at a law firm. I live here, but this isn't my place. It's my sister's."

"I didn't mean to pry," he removed his plaid jacket and hat. "But I know high-end living when I see it."

"My sister's a lawyer. She bought this townhouse seven or eight years ago." Jamila filled a small crystal vase with water, stuck the rose inside and placed it on the marble tile counter.

"She's getting married, so it'll be up for sale soon." Jamila picked up her bag and put on her jacket.

"Married? That's great." Nolan smiled and checked Jamila out from head-to-toe. "You ready?"

"I am."

Jamila entered Nolan's gray BMW 750 Li. She touched the charcoal gray leather armrest, scanning the innovative electronics playing studio clear music. *Amazing.* She chuckled to herself, *And I was worried about saving him money on our first dinner date.* She fastened her seat belt. "Beautiful car."

"A little gift to myself for working hard."

He pulled away from the curb, and Jamila felt him staring at her again. "Is everything okay?"

"It's all good, lady. I'm sorry for staring, I can't help being attracted to you." He glanced at her again and then looked back at the road. "You mind if we skip the Gospel Comedy Club and just do dinner?"

Jamila turned to Nolan. "If you have other plans, that's fine."

"Believe me, the only plan I have is to spend time with you." He placed his hand over hers.

His words sounded mushy, but they made Jamila feel special. A man with a kind heart who cared enough to spend time with her was more than she expected. Shifting in her seat, Jamila questioned if she was ready to date, and if so, would this lead to more than a friendship? The altercation with Otis was not the best first impression, but she dismissed the negative thoughts after considering how well Nolan stood up to Otis.

She hoped he was honest because she'd had enough one-night dates with little substance.

He admitted that he'd never been to the restaurant a friend recommended in Marina del Rey and asked Jamila for a second choice. She suggested another restaurant in Long Beach.

After the hostess seated them at Bubba Gump's, the waiter brought table settings, water, and menus.

Nolan opened the menu. "I didn't know they had Bubba Gump's out here. Living in California, I thought a romantic setting by the water would be cool for you."

"Not a bad idea when the weather's warm. But I can't take that breeze in the night air." Jamila looked around the restaurant, a large family was singing Happy Birthday to a young girl with a big bow in her hair.

Nolan bit his lower lip. "So, tell me about you."

"Sure," Jamila clasped her hands. "Then, I want you to do the same. I think I told you I went to Stanford. But what I didn't say was I dropped out during my last year. Three classes left."

"Wow. What happened?"

"My Grandma Ruth died." She shrugged. "Nothing seemed important after she was gone. She was my inspiration, the one who made me realize I could accomplish anything. At seventeen, I wasn't getting along with my mother, and my father was sick for a while. So, she shipped me off to South Carolina to live with Grandma Ruth for a year. I loved music, and so did she. And guess what? We both sang in the choir."

"Sorry to hear about your grandma. And I understand loving music."

"How did your father feel about your move?"

"My daddy? He wanted to keep peace in the house. I was rebellious and wrong. Told my mother I wasn't going to an HBCU and didn't care where my sister went to college," she said with a dismissive wave. Mama wanted her girls to keep the family tradition and go to HBCUs."

"That's not a negative thing. I never went to one, but I heard they're great."

"They are. My sister went off to Clark Atlanta, and then to law school. I wanted to study Music at Stanford. Mama wasn't having that. I finished high school, graduated and got accepted into Stanford."

"What are your major life goals, and do you plan to finish your degree?"

Jamila nodded. "I'll finish my classes online next semester. My other major life goals? To hear my songs on the radio, and I want to get married and have babies," she held her palms up. "Okay, I've told you a lot about me. Now, it's your turn."

"Whew. Marriage and babies. That's all cool when it's time."

The waiter brought appetizers, and they munched on shrimp cocktail and a variety of breads while Nolan discussed his musical career. He said he'd toured all over the United States, Europe, Africa, Central America, and Japan. He reiterated most of what he'd said the night before but didn't mention relationships with family or women and this concerned Jamila.

"So, have you ever been married? Do you have kids?" Jamila spread butter over a piece of sourdough bread.

Nolan's smile faded. "Good question. No, I've never been married. No kids, either." He gazed down at his glass and then slowly raised his head. "I truly want those things, though."

"What stopped you from having—"

"Can we change the topic?"

Jamila raised a brow. "Why? You can know about me," she pressed her hands against her chest, "but won't tell me about you."

"No. I mean...I will. Not now, but later."

Jamila lifted the napkin from her lap and pursed her mouth in a dissatisfied smirk. She hurled the napkin on the table and shook her head. "Unacceptable. It's unfair that you've talked about nothing but your career. I think we should leave."

"No, Jamila, please don't do this." He held out his arms. "I can explain."

"Okay, explain." She made eye contact, and his brown eyes shifted to the table again. Strange. This was certainly not what she expected. She was ready to call it a night, but she didn't want to make a hasty decision without exploring further.

Unable to figure him out, she offered a scant smile. "I'm a good listener. I have to know more about you. Otherwise, I can't see you again."

"I'm sure you are. Let's go to my place where we can have privacy."

She shook her head. "I won't do that."

"Sweetie, I know what you're thinking, and I understand." Nolan leaned over the table and squeezed Jamila's hand. "I've been through a lot, and my past is...complicated. I don't open up right away."

"You have to. How else can we get to know each other?"

"Honestly, I'm a cool person. Bishop wouldn't have hired me if I wasn't." He removed a handkerchief from his pocket and wiped beads of perspiration from his forehead. "Can we go to your place and chat? Or..." He looked around, "anywhere except here."

His tone and the plea on his face persuaded a change of heart. Deep inside, she sensed he was telling the truth. After all, he was the minister of music. "I'll go for that."

"Okay, I'll change our dinners to take out. Don't move. I'll go find the waiter." Nolan returned with two bags, paid the bill, and they left. When they arrived at the townhouse, Jamila tapped the security gate remote and he drove in.

"Turn left at the next block, then go straight. My sister's not here, so park in her stall next to my car. Jamila exited the car and noticed a blue paper stuck underneath the windshield wiper of her Honda. She snatched it off, the heat in her body rising. She read aloud, "You better watch your back, or you might come up missing. Ha, ha. From O.G."

Nolan frowned. "Let me see that." He read it again. "You know who left this on your car? That fool. I wish I could jam this down his throat for threatening you. And how did he get in the gate?"

Jamila smacked her lips. "He has the password, a backup for gate entry. We better get upstairs."

"I've got a better idea. Why don't you come to my place? This dude is apparently off his rocker, and he might be lurking around here. Show the note to your sister."

Jamila bent down and looked inside the car window, then peered over her shoulder, wondering if Otis was nearby. The note was clearly a threat, and now more than before, she believed her life was in imminent danger.

Chapter 5

Nolan had an immaculate, well-kept apartment in Culver City. The apartment was furnished with cocoa leather furniture and tons of interesting paintings and African-American sculptured figurines that brightened the environment. *Someday, I'll have a nice place of my own.*

"Make yourself at home," he dropped the bags on a round table surrounded by four chairs.

"Thank you." Jamila took a seat in a chair and glanced around. "Your place is cozy. The art is off the chain."

"Yeah, my personal treasures. Most of the art in here is from my travels. I'm into African-American art. This is a small portion of what was in my home. My Yamaha piano should arrive soon. You ready to eat?"

"I'm not sure I can," she brushed her hair from her face.

"I feel you. Who can eat or even think when some maniac is threatening you? Can I get you some juice, water, or a glass of wine?" He tossed his jacket on the couch. "Alexa, turn on the television."

"Hmmm, I don't drink often, but a glass of wine might calm my nerves."

Nolan went into the kitchen and came back with a bottle of Moscato and two wine glasses. "Thus far, we have some things in common," he said, pouring the wine. "Music and we don't drink often."

He reached out to her. She clasped his hand, rose, and moved over to the couch.

"What's with your ex?"

"Playing stupid games because I won't take him back."

He handed her the wine and sat next to her. "Well, I didn't want to bring this up during dinner, but I called Bishop Evans last night and told him what happened. Otis is out. He can't return to Mount Everest, but I'm worried about your safety."

"I'm worried, too. I know Otis. He's probably pissed off, especially about not being in the choir." Jamila sipped the wine and set the glass on a coaster. *How much more can I bear?* Otis blaming her for their breakup was wearing her down. She wanted her life back, but he was determined not to let that happen. She pulled her hands to her face as the tears flowed.

"Oh, baby, I'm sorry," Nolan removed a handkerchief from his jacket pocket. He dabbed her face and wrapped his arms around her shoulders. "Wish I could do more." He tipped her chin, and their eyes locked. "Just know I'm here, and I'll help you get through this." He planted his soft lips on hers and they kissed for what seemed like an eternity.

Having a sense of comfort had been unfamiliar for a long time, but his bulky arms provided safety and peace. They'd become so caught up with each other that discussing Nolan's history had become less important. A few glasses of wine later, Nolan told stories about some of the musicians who traveled with him on the road. She'd never laughed so hard.

"Stealing the hotel's towels and linen?" She laughed again.

"Yep. That's why I refused to share rooms." At half past 1:00 a.m., Nolan said, "It's time for bed. We have church tomorrow."

"Uh, uh." She clapped her forehead, feeling a bit woozy from the wine. "I forgot it's Saturday...or was. Wait, I can't go to church with you. I have to go home early."

"Calm down. I've got that squared away. I set my alarm," he rolled his wrist to recheck the time. "You can have my bed, and I'll sleep out here."

She lifted her hands. "You giving up your bed?"

"It's no big deal. I'll go find you a t-shirt to sleep in."

Wrapped up in her emotions, Jamila's mind played ping-pong about sleeping in Nolan's bed or on the couch. *His bedroom is personal.* Feeling more relaxed, she poured another glass of wine and sipped. *What if he had a girlfriend and she showed up?* No way. She finished the wine and walked to the bedroom to tell him she'd prefer the couch. He was sitting on the bed looking like a luscious lemon meringue pie with several t-shirts beside him.

"How many shirts you think I'ma wear?" She was woozy.

"I've been looking for a clean one. Here." He held up a blue short-sleeved shirt.

"Uh, I don't want to sleep in your bed." She waved him toward the door.

Nolan picked up his pajamas and walked toward the door laughing.

"Wait. I got that twisted. You're staying in here but give me a good-night hug first."

He opened his arms, and she sauntered over and fell into his embrace. He pulled her into a much-needed tight squeeze and held her. Enthralled with Nolan's warmth, smell, and touch, Jamila experienced temporary amnesia about all existing problems. She kissed his neck and tracked upward until her mouth found his. After unbuttoning his shirt, she raised her dress over her head, and it slid to the floor.

He backed up. "We shouldn't do this."

"Yes, we should."

Jamila slowly walked up to him and kissed his neck, he hoisted her in his arms, placed her on the bed, and showered her body with kisses. All she could think of was the sweet magic they had shared.

Jamila pried her eyes open to darkness, the aroma of food cooking generated flip-flops in her stomach. For a short period, she wondered if she was dreaming. She swung her legs to the floor and ran a hand along the bedside lamp to the switch. *Why am I in Nolan's bed? And where is my purse, my cell?* She glanced around and saw neither. Pressing a hand to her throbbing head, she snatched an aqua-blue terry cloth robe from a chair and stumbled to the kitchen.

"Hey, good morning, Madam. How'd you sleep?"

"Don't Madam me. How'd I get in your bed?"

He paused from stirring a bowl of eggs. "Come on now. You don't remember? We had wine and chatted for hours."

"I recall the wine. What I don't remember is getting in your bed. Oh, this is so embarrassing." She touched her forehead.

"Well, you did," he poured the eggs in a skillet and stirred, "after three glasses of wine."

"No, no, no. On occasion, I drink one glass. No more."

"Last night, you drank more. I was a little tipsy, too." He flipped sausages in a frying pan."

Leaning against the wall, her mind focused on Nolan. She barely knew him. Was he thinking bad thoughts? She should've followed her gut and stayed home, but it was too late for regrets.

"I'm sorry." Jamila assumed he'd disclose everything. Her mind was foggy, and she didn't want to believe that anything happened last night.

"No apologies necessary. I'm as much the blame as you." He placed two plates, silverware, and glasses of water and juice on the table. "We can make things right, though."

Jamila sat at the table. "Question. Did we—"

Nolan's gaze implied the worst news ever. She laid her throbbing head across folded arms and shut down. Neither said a word. How could she fix this fiasco?

"Make things right. How?" Jamila uttered in a soft voice.

"What I mean is...you won't believe me, but I'm falling in love with you," Nolan scooped eggs from the skillet. He placed the food on the table and sat across from Jamila. "I was smitten with you from the moment I walked in Mount Everest." He touched her arm. "I know we've crossed boundaries, but would you consider being my woman?"

She lifted her head; her mouth dropped open. "What the heck? You've gotta be joking. I bet you planned this."

"How could I?" He gave her an intense stare. "Hey, I get it. We just met. But, in your heart, do you really believe I'd set you up?"

Jamila threw her hands up. "I don't know what to believe. First, the note on my car. Now this. I didn't come here to sleep with you."

"And I didn't invite you here for that reason. I spoke from my heart. Now eat, I've gotta take you home."

Jamila wanted answers to fill in the blanks that she couldn't piece together. She was attracted to him, yet unsure about a committed relationship this early. "What time is it? I don't have my phone, purse, nothing. And I have a horrible hangover." Jamila rubbed her temples.

"It's 6:12. Alka-Seltzer is in the bathroom. Your stuff's in the closet near the chair. If you eat, you'll feel better."

"I won't feel better! What we did was outrageous," she snapped. She regretted going off and bowed her head. She had no right to be angry at anyone other than herself. "I'm a little edgy this morning." She searched Nolan's face as he ate and sipped coffee. His sudden change in demeanor alerted her that he was upset. "How could we let this happen so soon?"

"You're upset, and I feel bad. It won't happen again."

"Trust me, it won't," she glared at him.

"Baby, what else can I say? Look, let's pray." He reached for her hand.

Jamila quickly retracted her hand. "I can't." She got up and rushed to the bedroom and slammed the door. She slid the closet door open and found her purse and cell. Sitting on the edge of the chair, she dialed Chanelle.

"Girl, I been calling you."

Silence.

"Jamila, you there?"

Jamila sucked in a long breath like it was her last, then exhaled. "I slept with Nolan. We'll talk later."

Chapter 6

Jamila lifted her head. Never again would she drink anymore alcohol. The Alka-Seltzer was beginning to work, but she didn't feel much better.

She couldn't believe she'd slept this late, and wanted to kick herself for going to bed with Nolan. This meant staying on her knees in daily prayer for a lifetime. *Lord, please forgive me.* She threw back the cover and unplugged her cell. Four calls from Nolan, two texts from Chanelle and one said, *Urgent. Call ASAP!!!* She put on her robe, walked to the kitchen for a bottled water and tapped Chanelle's number.

"It's about time. What happened to you today?"

"I didn't feel well. It's not a sin to miss church."

"Layin' up with the minister of music is. What got into you?"

"Don't start. I've got a hangover. I'm mad and still trying to figure out what happened last night." She sat on a stool near the counter and turned up the water bottle, guzzling half.

"Whatever. Can you stop by today? We've gotta talk. Our recording session and audition was pushed back a month."

"A month? That's a bad sign. When did you find out?"

"Today after church. There's more to the story. I'll update you."

"Give me an hour and I'm on my way." *Now what?* Hopefully, all the effort and hard work they'd put forth hadn't been in vain.

Celeste walked into the kitchen. "You didn't go to church?"

"I didn't feel well, so I slept in."

She laughed. "Too much fun last night?"

If CeCe knew the truth, she'd do one-hundred somersaults, then call our mother and she'd do the same. "Yep, but I'll be fine. Going to Chanelle's, then I'm resting."

"Okay. I received your text. I'm filing the restraining order tomorrow, so I'll talk to you later. Where's the note?"

"On the dresser."

"I'll get it. I'm going to lunch. Oh, Mama invited us to dinner. Consider inviting your friend."

"Is she and Daddy back already?"

Celeste cut her eyes. "No, Jami, they've only been in Las Vegas two days. They'll be back Wednesday. See you later."

Jamila showered, dressed, and ate a piece of toast to reduce the nausea that lingered. Although the hangover hadn't fully subsided, meeting Chanelle was important.

She parked in front of Chanelle's house and scurried up the driveway. Before she reached the door, she heard her friend's voice.

"Come on in."

Jamila entered as Chanelle exited the kitchen. "Well dang, how'd you know I was here?"

"New security cameras. Darius took the kids to the park." She handed a folder to Jamila.

"What's this?"

"Take a seat, read the article first, and then the flyer."

Jamila's brows furrowed after she finished. "This is insane. I didn't know Alexander Wayne went to prison for murder."

"Think about it. When's the last time he put out a record? And I'm curious about his backup singers, Soldiers in Christ."

"I don't know."

"Now read the flyer," Chanelle crossed her legs. "Most of the choir got the flyer last night in an email."

As Jamila read, she covered her mouth. "No, this can't be true. Nolan's not Alexander Wayne. I mean, Alexander is a big man."

"Take a closer look. He lost weight, shaved his beard and cut his hair. That's him."

"Who sent this stuff?" she frowned. "Do you really have to ask? Everybody thinks Otis did. One of the choir members saw him this morning."

"Please don't mention him." She felt extra sick after reading the information. Maybe that's the reason they postponed the recording session. And poor Nolan must be devastated. If he'd been through this and was still standing, he had to be strong and faithful.

"You know you can't drink. And I'm surprised about you and Brother Nolan."

"Trust me, it wasn't intentional," Jamila pressed a hand against her head. "My hangover will make me think twice about alcohol. The man tried to protect me. I found a threatening note on my car, and he suggested I go to his place. When I woke up in his bed, I went off on him." She glanced at Chanelle. "He apologized. I can't believe I treated him that way."

"I could tell Brother Nolan was upset today. Whoever leaked his identity was wrong. Bishop Evans even addressed it during service. He told us to tear up all those flyers and not let the devil create havoc. I saved mine to show you. The man did four years in prison and he was innocent."

Jamila slipped on her jacket and picked up her purse.

"You leaving?"

"Yes, I misjudged Nolan. I need to go find my man."

Chanelle raised a brow. "Which man?"

"Nolan," Jamila said with a broad smile. "This morning, he asked if I'd be his woman, and then asked me to pray with him."

"Go after him, girl."

Chapter 7

Inhaling and exhaling a deep breath, Jamila exited her car and set the alarm. She paused to consider if she should ring Nolan's apartment for entry. *I will do this. I will go in, apologize, and tell him how much I care about him.* A woman holding a toddler in her arms exited the building and held the door open for Jamila to enter.

Jamila tapped on Nolan's door.

He opened it, and his eyes widened. "Jamila, what are you doing here?"

"I came to see you. Are you busy?"

"No, come in," he threw a roll of tape on the table. "I'm packing a few things. What's up?"

"You tell me," she surveyed the rows of boxes against the wall. "Are you moving?" She sat on the couch, and he sat next to her.

"I'm meeting with Bishop tomorrow. I'd planned to discuss my past last night."

"Is that why you're leaving?"

His gaze met hers. "You know?"

She nodded. "There's no reason to leave. You were exonerated."

"The point is, it's not working." He brushed a finger over his mustache. "After I got out of prison six years ago, I changed my name, figured I could revive my career." He bit his lower lip and stared into space. "Everywhere I moved, people found out about me, and I'd leave. I was known as Alexander Wayne, the convict. I got judged and ridiculed for being a murderer." He shook his head. "I'm not, but prison gave me time to reflect on my life. And, I asked the Lord to give me another chance to serve Him. My mom had handled all my finances, and I still had my assets when I got out. I knew I would sing again."

"That must've been hard."

He nodded. "It was. Before I went to prison, I was Alexander Wayne, Stellar Award winner, at the top of my game. Then, I got involved with a married woman. Well, I didn't know she was married, but I cut ties when I discovered it. Didn't matter, she kept showing up at my concerts.

One night, she showed up at my place. Her husband followed and went ballistic. He started punching and kicking her." Nolan's fists balled. "I had to stop him. When I did, he pulled out a gun, we wrestled, the gun went off and a bullet hit his stomach. He died later at the hospital."

"Nolan, I had no idea. You could've talked to me. I don't judge anybody because I'm sure you know I'm not perfect. I've struggled with self-esteem and anger management but thank God I'm much better."

"You weren't in church today. I assumed you wouldn't see me again after last night."

"Look at me," Jamila reached for his hands. "I was angry at myself about last night. And I shouldn't have lashed out at you. On another note, instead of running away, why not pray and fight? If people can't accept you...oh, well. That's their problem. We need you at Mount Everest. I need you. As your woman, I'll stand beside you."

A smile brightened his face. "Thank you, Sweetie, that means a lot to me. I'm definitely not going anywhere now." He ran a finger across her cheek. "Can I ask you something?"

"Of course."

He sighed. "Do you believe in love at first sight?"

"I do now."

"Awesome. Next, we'll work on those goals, especially marriage and babies." He pulled her to his chest, they embraced, and his lips brushed hers.

About the Author

Reading and daily journal entries were the catalyst to Patricia's first novel, *Reflections of a Quiet Storm*, published by an independent publisher in 2009. An avid reader, her previous published work includes two books, multiple short stories, monthly health care columns for an online magazine, and several health care articles for a local newspaper. She also enjoys reading women's fiction and romance novels, which occupy many seats on her bookshelves.

Patricia is a Family Nurse Practitioner and a Psychiatric-Mental Health Nurse Practitioner, she holds Adjunct Nursing Faculty positions at two universities. She is a member of the National Black Nurses Association/Council of Black Nurses – L.A., Sigma Theta Tau International Honor Society of Nursing, Black Nurses Rock, California Association of Nurse Practitioners, and International Black Writers & Artists. Patricia's church home is West Angeles Church of God in Christ in Los Angeles. She considers music, reading, and prayer as the keys to relaxation and creativity, and she loves spending time with her family.

Patricia's short story appears in the Brown Girls Books Anthology, *Single Mama Dating Drama*, an AALBC two-time best-selling book. *Two Steps Past the Altar* is her third and latest novel. She is currently working on her fourth novel.

Visit her online at patriciabridewell.com

Love Walked In

Unlikely Companions
Alicia Fleming

Eden heard laughter, a shrill, rowdy cacophony of laughter. She looked up from the paperwork she was finishing, "Ashley, is everything okay?"

"Yes, ma'am, I was just laughing at Mr. Sharon's jokes."

Eden pushed back from the desk and went to the sales counter. She smirked at Ashley's blushing. *Nothing is that funny,* Eden thought to herself.

"Ashley, why don't you pull the weekly report since it is Friday, and I will take care of Mr. Sharon." Dismissing her sales manager, Eden turned to the gentleman. "Mr. Sharon, is there something in particular you are looking for?"

The man stood to his full height and smiled. Eden noticed his athletic build and beautiful set of pearly white teeth. *Wow, no wonder the girl was laughing like that.*

With a slight shake of the head, he said. "No, I can't afford anything in here, but... Well, maybe one day, I will be able to shop in your store. One of these suits cost more than I make in a week or two, even the ones on sale," he chuckled.

For the first time, Eden noticed the UPS emblem on his brown work uniform. She smiled. "Well, they are tailor made, but we do try to work with any budget to give our customers what they want. Besides, you really should treat yourself every now and then."

He looked at her and smiled. "Maybe one day."

The man was attractive. Eden had to give him that, but she didn't date men who were not in her income bracket. They had to make what she was making or more. She knew her standards were extremely high, but she had seen too many women settle for the first thing that came along, and she didn't want that to be her. Eden refused to be another statistic where the man brought nothing into the marriage and left with half of the money she had earned. She was not going out like that and she meant it. Her and her best friend, Anya had built this high-end men's clothing store from the ground up, and it had grown like wildfire in the last five years. Their store attracted business executives, athletes, doctors and pillars of the community, and if the fine man in the brown uniform couldn't afford a suit from her shop, she knew he couldn't afford her.

"Well, I say we get Ashley to notify you when we have our next sale."

He smiled, "Why don't you notify me of the next sale?"

"I'm sorry. Are you flirting with me, Mr. Sharon?"

"You can't blame a brother for trying, now can you?"

"No, I can't." *But, brother, you can't even afford to take me out for a nice dinner.* Eden returned the smile. "Well, I have some work to finish up, so why don't you leave your information with Ashley and we will be in touch."

He turned to leave but looked back over his shoulder. "By the way, my name is Bryce, tell the owner I like this store and I will be back."

"I will do that," Eden nodded, laughing to herself. These male chauvinists are going to get enough of underestimating women.

Eden's phone rang. She knew by the ringtone it was her business partner and BFF, Anya. "Hello."

"Hey, girl. How's it going in the store today?"

"It's going okay. I just had a UPS driver flirt with me. He was cute, but you know he's not on my level."

"You could at least give the man a try, Eden, he may be nice."

"Aaaahhh, no thank you." Eden laughed. "Girl, you know I need some stimulating conversation and someone who knows how to treat a lady."

"Eden, you are being presumptuous. He may be a great catch."

"Whatever, Anya. Then maybe you should go out with him."

"Negative, my black book is filling up fast."

"Girl, you are crazy," Eden laughed. "How are things going with the condo?"

After Anya and Eden's retail store became profitable, the ladies purchased a limousine, obtained their commercial driver's license and started a limo service. For their latest entrepreneurial endeavor, they had expanded into real estate and hit the market at the right time. They'd purchased when the market was down and did very well flipping properties. Recently, they had acquired a condominium building and were leasing out the units.

"We're finishing up paperwork now so I should be by the store shortly," Anya informed her.

"Don't bother. I'm finishing up the books and headed home, so do your thing. What are you up to tonight?" Eden asked.

"I have a date."

"Really, with who?"

"You don't know him. He's new."

"Well, I can't wait to hear if this new him passes the first date test."

Anya and Eden had always been best friends. They'd grown up together in an upper middle-class neighborhood in Nashville called Green Hills. The area had a high-end mall, great restaurants and some beautiful homes. They attended Franklin Road Academy, and then matriculated to Howard University together. Howard was a different world for the sisters whose private school were comprised of nineteen percent diversity. After college, they traveled the world together visiting exotic places like Bora Bora, Tanzania and Tahiti. Neither of them wanted to depend on men for their well-being, but that's where the similarities ended. Eden wanted to settle down one day with one man and have a family. Anya, on the other hand, enjoyed playing the field. And, Eden loved the fact that her BFF was like the guys, she could love them and leave them, and she didn't take any crap off of men. A Lena Horne lookalike who knew how to work her magic and get what she wanted, she decided if there would be a second date. Growing up, Anya got all of the guys' attention, and years later, she was still getting it.

"What about you?" Anya asked.

"Me? I'm probably going to pour me a glass of wine and chill. I have been running hard for a few weeks and a sistah could use some rest." Eden looked at her watch and signaled for Ashley to lock the door. "Have a great time on your date, sis. I'll talk to you tomorrow. Love you, be careful."

"Love you too," Anya said before disconnecting the call.

It was only 7:30. *This is ridiculous,* Eden thought to herself. *I can't go home this early on a Friday night.* "Ashley, do you want to go hang out for a while?"

"I can for a little while, but I have a date later. What did you have in mind?"

"Martinis, my treat."

"You're the boss." Ashley said with a hair flip.

They arrived at one of the local spots called Green Hills Grille and took a seat at a high-top table in the bar area. Before they could place their order, the waitress brought over two martinis. "Ladies, the gentleman at that table sent these martinis over."

Ashley and Eden looked over at the table. It was the UPS guy that was in the store earlier. Ashley's face broke into a wide grin.

"Stop that," Eden said.

"What? The man looks good and that body... Hmmm."

"Really, Ashley? You sound like you're in your twenties or thirties."

"Well, I am and I know what I like," Ashley exclaimed.

The guy waved his hand at the ladies and turned back to his conversation with the other gentleman at his table.

"Girl, I saw him in that uniform. He delivering packages, ain't nothing he can do for me."

"Wow, Eden, he may be a really nice guy, and you're just going to dismiss him because he doesn't wear designer suits and make over six figures. He might be one of the nicest men you'll ever meet."

Eden folded her arms. "He may be, but I'm not willing to chance it. I want a brother already on my level or almost there. I need a man with vision, someone already established. I don't want to explain why I have to work or fly off to New York for a quick meeting. My man needs to know how to wine and dine with my clients and future business partners. I don't want to have to teach someone which fork to use at a dinner party or buy him a tux to wear for dinner because he doesn't already own one. I don't have the time or the energy to do all of that."

"Well, you probably have someone right in your face that you keep looking past. Remember, it's not about the outside of the package but what's inside the package."

"Yea, like a brain." Eden quipped.

Ashley shook her head. "Look, I better get out of here so I can go change for this cutie pie. I'll see ya tomorrow, boss."

"Enjoy your date, Ash. I'm gonna go enjoy my peace and quiet and wine."

Before leaving, the ladies hugged goodbye, and Ashley turned to give the kind gentleman who paid for their drinks one last smile. Eden glanced in the man's direction and then walked out to the car service waiting to take her to her penthouse. *Owning your own limo company has its privileges,* she thought to herself as she slipped into the back seat.

At home, Eden settled into something comfortable and poured herself a glass of wine. Unamused by the movie on her television, she picked up her phone. There was a message notification about a meeting in New York City on Monday with a new client. *Dang!* She smacked her hand against her forehead.

"Darn, I forgot to put that on my calendar. Bet I won't be able to find a first-class seat on any flight this late." Eden started making phone calls, finally she was able to get a flight on a private jet for early Monday morning. "Whoo, thank God money is no object. If this deal goes through, I am going to take off for a month and go hang out in Italy."

Tense from all the stress, Eden decided to go for a run. She needed to release some of the pent-up anxiety in her body. She changed into her running gear and did some light stretches before putting on her music. Normally, she'd run on her treadmill or go to the gym, but tonight, she felt like being outside and started running down West End.

Halfway through her run, she felt a sharp pain in her side. "Good gosh," Eden said trying to draw a deep breath. She figured it was just a catch that would pass and kept running. When the pain hit the second time, she stopped and doubled over. The pain was so intense, Eden thought she was going to pass out. She could feel herself getting lightheaded, and then she heard someone say, "Hey, lady, are you alright?"

"I'm, I'm not sure," was all she managed to say before everything went black.

Eden woke up in the hospital with Anya sitting in a chair beside her bed.

She looked around. "Where am I? What are you doing here? What happened?"

"Girl, don't scare me like that. I got a phone call saying you had been rushed to the hospital. You had an appendicitis attack, and they had to do emergency surgery on you. Thank God that guy in the park was there to get you some help."

"Are you serious? What guy? Who called you?"

"Don't worry about it, you are going to be taking it easy the next few weeks so you may as well get ready to sit back and relax."

"I don't have time to sit back and relax. I have a meeting Monday morning in New York and a full week ahead."

"Oh well, that's not happening. I'll go to the meeting in New York, and I can get Ashley to run the store and the limo service while you are recuperating."

Eden and Anya continued to banter back and forth about her resting until a knock on the door interrupted them. The door opened slowly.

"Some things never change," the man entering the room chuckled. "What are you two fussing about?"

Eden stared at the guy. He looked familiar, and she kind of recognized the voice, but for the life of her, she couldn't place him. She looked at Anya who was staring at the guy as well. *No help there.*

"Don't tell me y'all have forgotten a brother after all these years. It's me, Kingsley. I'm the guy that called 911 for you in the park. After I heard them say your name, I knew it had to be you."

"Oh my God, Kingsley! It's been twenty plus years since we've seen you," Eden said. "I can't believe this. What in the world have you been doing with yourself?"

Eden wanted to hear his answer, but she couldn't manage to keep her eyes open. When she drifted off to sleep, Anya started laughing. "She is going to be so embarrassed that you have seen her at her worse without makeup."

"Right," Kingsley laughed, "like I haven't seen that before."

Anya shook her head. "I can't believe you saved Eden's life."

"I didn't recognize her at first, but when the paramedics asked her to identify herself and she said her name, I knew it had to be her. There aren't many people named Eden, so I decided to come and wait at the hospital to see if I could find out anything. Then, I saw you and followed you up here. I kept my distance at first because I wasn't sure if it was you, your hair is a different color and much shorter than I remember."

"Well, you look different as well. I'm pretty sure you had hair the last time we saw you."

"Really? That's what you are going to start off with, Anya?"

"What in the world have you been doing all these years? You may as well start talking, I will be here all night to make sure my girl is okay."

Eden slept peacefully as Anya and Kingsley played catch up.

When Eden finally stirred, the morning sun was shining into her hospital room. She blinked her eyes in disbelief. She had expected Anya in the chair next to her bed not Kingsley.

"Hold on now, superwoman, take it easy." Kingsley stood to assist her.

"What are you still doing here?" Eden asked.

"I told Anya to go home since she had been here all night. She went to shower and get you some pajamas. You know that hospital gown is way too sexy for you."

Eden laughed. "I see you still have your sense of humor." She looked down at the bed before looking back at him. "You look great, by the way. I like your look — the bald head and the goatee. I've often wondered what happened to you after..."

"Likewise, I always wondered what happened to you and Anya, but I can't believe we are here under these circumstances."

Eden grabbed Kingsley's hand. "Thank you. I can't believe you saved my life."

"I only did what any kindhearted human being would do in an emergency. Too bad I didn't have to give you mouth to mouth," he grinned sheepishly.

Eden wasn't sure how to feel about seeing him again, but he looked great and all she could think about was the fact that she was lying in bed with no makeup on. Kingsley had always been easy to talk too, and he didn't seem to mind her bare face. From their love of music to failed relationships and crazy folks they had dated over the years, they spent the morning catching up.

Kingsley had been interested in politics, and Eden had no desire to be a politician's wife. She and Anya had a plan, and she was focused on her business goals... and her daughter. Fed up with waiting on her then boyfriend to pop the question, Eden had planned her pregnancy. The night she was going to tell him that she was pregnant, he confessed that he had gotten his ex-girlfriend pregnant. Eden thought she would die from heartbreak. Other than building her business with Anya, this man had been her entire world, and she worshipped the ground he walked on. She adored his family and her family adored him. A few weeks after his big confession, they met for dinner, and he told her that he loved her and wanted them to still be together. She remembered it like it was yesterday. "What foolishness, I'm in love with him and pregnant and he just had a baby with his ex-girlfriend," she had whined to Anya.

She made the decision not to tell him that she was pregnant. After they finished dinner, Eden told him that she loved him, but she was not going to compete with another woman for his love and affection and she wouldn't compete with his child. She kissed him and walked out and never saw him again. She went through the pregnancy with the support of her family and her bestie, Anya, and delivered a beautiful little girl named Sasha.

When Anya accidentally became pregnant, she too had a beautiful little girl and named her Simone. Eden and Anya raised their girls together, deciding they would do what was best for their girls and keep it moving. Eden backed off from dating and concentrated on her daughter and her business. But, it was easy with Kingsley because he was raising his son as a single parent as well. When they dated, they let their kids play together, and the three of them would babysit for one another and often have dinner together. He and Eden parted ways when he decided to focus on politics and, somehow or another, lost each other's numbers. Over the years, she'd often wondered what happened to the man she'd been so close to. Now, here he was sitting in her hospital room. He had saved her life, like literally saved her life.

"Kingsley, how is your mom?"

He froze for a moment. "My mom went to be with the Lord about a year after..."

"I'm so sorry, Kingsley. Why didn't you call me?" She reached for his hand. "I'm sorry, that was a stupid question. You were grieving, but you know I would have been there for you." She told him about her mom, and they sat in silence holding each other's hands.

The door flung open. Anya looked at the two of them holding hands and started smiling. "Uhh, what is going on in here?" Anya asked.

They quickly moved their hands apart and grinned at each other.

Kingsley stood and looked at Eden. "Well, lovely ladies, I need to be going. We'll continue playing catch up soon. Eden, please behave yourself while you're here."

She nodded, "I'll try my best, but you know that's no fun."

He handed her his business card and bent to kiss her on top of the forehead. "Don't lose that card, and don't let it be another twenty years before we talk again."

Eden felt herself blushing and looked at Anya who was grinning like a cat that swallowed the canary.

"What are you grinning about, Anya?" Eden asked her after Kingsley left the room.

"Did I interrupt something?"

"No, you didn't," Eden smiled.

Anya smirked. "Yea, right."

"We were just playing catch up. A lot has happened in twenty years; we're two different people now." Eden looked out the hospital window, she wondered if she would see Kingsley again.

The Next Day

"I am so ready to go home. I can't stay here another day." Eden told her daughter on the phone. Someone knocked on her door. "Hey, honey, I have to go. Someone's at the door, love you."

"Come in," Eden yelled. A huge bouquet of flowers came through the door with Kingsley following behind.

"Girl, are you in here causing trouble?"

She shook her head. "No, I'm not."

Her nurse looked Kingsley up and down. "Well, I think I will let you two chat, and I will come back a little later." She winked at Eden before leaving the room.

"Kingsley, what in the world?"

He shrugged. "Beautiful flowers for a beautiful lady, that's all."

"You are so sweet. Thank you so much." Eden wasn't sure what to think.

"You're something else, you know that?"

She nodded. "Yea, I kinda know that."

Kingsley chuckled. "So, when are you being released?"

"Hopefully, sometime today. Sasha is coming to pick me up since Anya has been holding down the business while I've been here."

"Well, I hope that I'm still here to meet Sasha if that's okay with you?"

"I don't mind at all. In fact, I wanted to ask you about your son the other day. How old is he now?"

"Grown with a family of his own."

"So, you're a grandpa?" Eden shook her head. "Too funny."

"What's so funny about me being a grandpa?"

"I don't know, but I'm sure you're an amazing grandpa just like you were an amazing dad."

"I hope so. I always strived to be a great role model for my son, you know."

Eden was caught up in Kingsley's smooth light brown skin and dark eyes. She was a sucker for a good-looking man. "So, Kingsley, what are you doing with yourself these days?"

"I run a nonprofit that helps men get back into society after being in prison. We help them find employment, work on getting their college degree or trade certificate, and of course, we minister to them. Many of them have horrible backgrounds and have never known a mother or father's encouragement. Without solid support systems, these men ended up making bad decisions that led them to prison. Some of them end up turning their lives around and some don't. I help the ones I can and keep it moving."

"You have always had a calling on your life and a heart to serve others, Kingsley. I admire your tenacity to help folks. I'm sure the guys you've helped adore you."

"I don't know if I would use the word 'adore' but..." They both laughed.

Eden hadn't really missed being at work. She didn't realize how tired her body was. The nurse told her that she had been sleeping a lot and when they released her, she should go home and finish recuperating. They wanted her to take it easy for a few more weeks, but Eden wasn't one of those people who could sit still very long, so this recovery process was going to be a thorn in her side.

The door to her room flung open as she and Kingsley continued to converse. Sasha rushed in, "Hey, Mom," she stopped short, "Oh, I'm sorry. I didn't realize you had company."

"No, come on in, baby. Sasha, this is my friend Kingsley. Kingsley – Sasha."

"Well, hello, young lady, you're just as beautiful as your mom."

"Hello," Sasha said.

"I know you don't remember me, but you, Simone and my son used to play together when you all were around three years old."

Sasha blushed. "You're right, I don't remember. Sorry." She turned to her mom, "But, they called and told me that I could pick up this patient named Eden who has been causing trouble at the hospital, so I dropped by and I'm glad I did so I could meet you."

Kingsley laughed. "Yes, your mother is a handful, isn't she? Always has been, but you call me if she gives you any trouble once she gets home. I'm going to head out, Eden. It was great seeing you all grown up, Sasha. What are you doing with yourself?"

"I am a lawyer at Bass Berry & Sims, one of the firms downtown."

"Really? I bet your mother didn't tell you that I also have a law degree."

"No, I didn't know that. Apparently, there's a lot she hasn't told me," Sasha raised her eyebrow and looked at her mother.

"Well, Eden, I will let this young lady get you home so you can get some rest. I'll call and check on you later."

"Wait, you don't have my number." Eden said.

"Oh yea, I do, Anya gave it to me. Get some rest." Kingsley leaned over and kissed her on the forehead before saying goodbye.

The minute the door closed, Sasha asked, "Mom, who was that?"

"What do you mean, Sasha?"

"What do I mean? Mom, who was that fine man in here talking to you and kissing you on your forehead? I can't leave you and Anya alone for any amount of time without men flocking to you."

"Kingsley is an old friend, and believe it or not, he's the one that saved my life."

"Well, he's a nice looking old friend. Where did these flowers come from?"

"You sure are nosy, young lady."

"Oh, so they are from him as well?" Sasha snapped her fingers. "Ah shucks now as Nanny used to say."

"Girl, sit down and help me get ready to get out of here."

"Are you going to see Kingsley again?"

"I don't know, Sasha." Eden cocked her head. "You are all up in my business."

"Well, somebody needs to be. All you do is work, Mom, and you should be able to have someone pay attention to you. I know you don't date a lot because you throw yourself into your work and you have such high standards, but sometimes what you need is right in front of you. It may not always be packaged the way you want it but remember what you told me. It's all about the heart."

Eden laughed. "When did you get so smart?"

Sasha put her hands on her hips. "Are you taking your own advice?"

"Sometimes," Eden laughed.

Her daughter shook her head. "Let's get you out of here. This hospital attire is not cute. You know we have to be cute even when we're laid up."

Sasha took Eden home and helped her settle into her bedroom. She had the house cleaned, plenty of food in the fridge, and some fresh fruit.

"I hope everything is okay for you, Mom. I'm going to stay here for a few nights, I don't want you to need anything."

"You don't have to do that, Sasha."

"Yes, I do. If I don't, you will be up working and all over the place."

"You and Anya are going to drive me batty with all of this fussing over me."

"You deserve it, Mom, now get in your bed and surf the channels or read a good book."

"Yes, mother," Eden said sarcastically.

"Well, don't let me have to tell you again then. You know what happens in this house when you don't mind, you get a whoopin."

They both burst into laughter. Sasha sounded exactly like Eden use to sound when Sasha was smaller and Eden had to reprimand her. She couldn't believe how fortunate she was to have this amazing daughter. She often thought about telling Sasha's dad about her, but the timing never seemed right. When Sasha got older, she told Sasha about their relationship and what had happened. She wanted Sasha to feel free to reach out to her dad or she would for her, but Sasha never did. Eden didn't want her daughter to be angry or bitter toward men. She thought Sasha would have been angry with her, but when she explained everything, Sasha said she didn't blame her for the choice she made.

It was nice to be home and relax without worrying about the business. Eden purposed in her heart to send Anya on an amazing trip when she went back to work. She was grateful for her partner and BFF holding down all of their enterprises while she was recuperating. Thank God for their protégé Ashley being a fast learner.

She was so much more than a sales manager for their retail store and definitely about to get a promotion. Anya and Eden both recognized her as an asset to their business, and they loved her like she was their little sister. Eden sighed and flipped through the book she was trying to read. She had read the same page four times, and each time her mind would drift to the business. Her phone rang.

"Hello."

"Hey, beautiful, how are you?"

She smiled. "Hey, Kingsley, I'm fine and you?"

"I'm good. I can't complain. How are you feeling?"

"I'm feeling better, but I'm about to go stir crazy in this house. Anya and Sasha are like two mother hens and they won't let me do anything. The doctor told me I could get out and about but those two are like bodyguards."

"Well, I have the rest of the day clear, you want to go to the park or have lunch?"

Eden was speechless. "Sure, why not. I would love to get some fresh air."

She showered and put on some clothes and did her hair and makeup. "It's amazing what a few weeks of rest will do for your skin." An hour later, her doorbell rang.

"Who is it?" Eden asked.

"Who are you expecting?" asked a voice on the other side. "Would you buzz me in so I can come up to see you?" Kingsley laughed. "I didn't know a brother was going to have to go through all of this to come see you. I'm surprised I didn't get frisked."

As the elevator opened up to her penthouse, Kingsley stood there looking great.

"Hey, you." Kingsley smiled at her.

"Hey, come on in. I'm almost ready. I just need to put on my shoes and grab my purse."

He grabbed her and gave her a hug. "You're looking good."

"Thank you," Eden blushed.

"Wow, your place is amazing, Eden. I love the layout and the color scheme."

"Thanks. I did it myself."

"I see you still have your music collection."

"And you know it," she said. "What about you?"

"Yep, same here. Nothing like some good music – it's classic." He reached for her hand. "Shall we go, my lady?"

"Sure, let's do it."

Lunch was filled with conversation about where they were in life with their careers, their children, family, et cetera. With the exception of both of them losing their mothers, it felt like she and Kingsley had never lost touch with one another.

"So, Kingsley, did you ever get married?"

He shook his head. "No, never found the right one. I dated some, but I was never the lady's man you thought I was."

"Yea right, Kingsley, women tend to throw themselves at you."

"Yea, all of them but you. You just walked out of my life."

"No, I knew you had goals you wanted to reach, and as much fun as you and I had, I wasn't ready for a serious relationship at the time. I didn't think you were either. We never really talked about it much. It was like you, me and Anya were each other's support system. When you said you were going into politics, that just wasn't something I was interested in, so I bounced. Then one day I was looking for your number and couldn't find it anywhere. By the time Anya and I came back to your apartment, you were gone. She was crazy about your roommate, and I thought they would have hung out for a while, but it was like we all stopped seeing each other at the same time and just dropped off the face of the earth. I always wondered what happened to you, but I didn't have a way to find you. I knew you would do something great with your life. I kept watching for you as the new up and coming politician.

"Well, I thought I would be able to change the world, but all I did was get burnt out. I decided to change things one person at a time. I raised my son and then started my nonprofit... I love what I'm doing." Kingsley shared his success stories and some of the ones that weren't so successful.

"You can only do so much, Kingsley. I think what you're doing is great."

"Well, it's not as exciting as what you and Anya have going on, but it pays my bills." Eden caught herself looking at Kingsley differently. They were both more mature now and really knew what they wanted in life.

"Eden, why aren't you married?"

"Same reason. I threw myself into my child and my career. Decided I didn't have time for love and getting my heart shattered into a million pieces again. After dating someone as long as Sasha's dad and I were together and have it end disastrously, and then have another failed relationship years later, that was enough for me. I figured I was the problem, but then I realized that I wasn't. I just dated guys that ended up taking me for granted. I think they loved me as best they could, but they didn't appreciate me. So, I love myself, spoil myself and my child and live a nice comfortable life. Sure, there are times I wish I had someone to go out with or go to the movies or museum, but that's where my girls come in. I'm not about settling ever again. If a guy can't treat me the way I want to be treated, then I will stay single." Eden watched Kingsley watching her, but he didn't seem to be with her. "Kingsley, did you hear me?"

"I'm sorry, I was caught up in my thoughts. I didn't mean to be rude."

They stayed out most of the day walking, talking, eating ice cream. Kingsley even took her out to Radnor Lake where they enjoyed a picnic and talked and laughed until their sides and faces hurt.

While laughing, Eden caught a glimpse of her phone. She'd missed several calls from Anya and Sasha.

"You better call them back before they call the police and report you missing," Kingsley laughed. He had an infectious laugh that made Eden want to laugh as well.

Eden knew Anya and Sasha had been worried about her. She called Sasha who gave her the third degree. "I'm fine," she reassured her daughter. She called Anya who also gave her the third degree. "Both you and Sasha stop worrying, I'm in good hands." She smiled at Kingsley. Anya yelled in the background, "Tell Kingsley I said hello and to get you back home."

"Bye, girl." Eden hung up the phone.

Kingsley stood. "I better get you back home. I didn't mean to keep you out this long, but it has been so much fun hanging out and talking with you."

"If we must."

"Yep, let's go." Kingsley opened the door for her, and she got back into his immaculate black Jaguar. Eden admired his glistening wheels, the all black leather interior and brand new car smell. *He always did have great taste in cars.*

Kingsley was such a gentleman. When they arrived back at Eden's penthouse, he escorted her to her door.

"Well, I think both of the mother hens have gone back to their nest. Would you like to come in or are you headed home?"

"If I could have some water before I leave, that would be great."

She laughed and handed him a glass of water, "You know this is like old times. After the first visit, you're no longer considered a guest. So, the next time you are here, you can get your own water."

He nodded and took the glass, "Hmmm, well that sounds like I might get invited back. Is that what you're saying?"

She looked at him and grinned, before walking him to the door. "Thanks so much for rescuing me again."

"Well, can a brother get a hug since I rescued you again?"

Eden hugged him and inhaled his cologne. Their embrace lingered as Eden remembered what it was like to be held in a warm embrace that only a man could give.

Kingsley came again the next week and took her out so they could spend the day together. They continued going to the park, taking long strolls and talking about life as if they had never missed a beat with one another. Kingsley often held her hand while they walked and talked for what seemed like forever. Everything felt so right when Eden was with Kingsley, but she was hesitant and unsure about where all of this was going.

One day, after a stroll and an ice cream cone, Kingsley gave her a hug. They broke the embrace but not their gaze, and the next thing Eden knew they were kissing passionately. At one point, Eden thought she stopped breathing. She had forgotten about Kingsley's serious lip and tongue action, and he still had it. Eden loved to kiss and could feel herself melting ounce by ounce as the kiss deepened. She wondered if Kingsley could feel her heart beating through her shirt. When they pulled apart, Eden felt things rise in her body that she hadn't felt in a long time.

"Wow," They both said at the same time.

Kingsley ran his hand over his bald head. "I'm sorry. I should have asked you first if I could do that but being with you all day just felt good. I really didn't mean to kiss you, but you looked so beautiful, I couldn't help myself."

"Trust me, Kingsley, I enjoyed every moment of that kiss."

As before, Kingsley saw her safely home, and before they knew it, they were kissing again. It was like they couldn't get enough of each other. As their mouths and bodies pressed together, Eden could feel her temperature rising and other things within her and within Kingsley.

He broke the kiss and hugged her tight, "I missed you more than I realized; I better go." She blushed, wanting him to stay longer.

"I hope you had a great time today and hopefully, we can do it again real soon," he cleared his throat. "Er...uh... I mean get together real soon." He kissed the top of her forehead and smiled before walking out the door. Eden wanted to melt onto the floor. What in the world? Her phone rang bringing her out of her trance.

"Eden, did Kingsley get you back home?" Anya interrogated.

"Oh yea, yea, he did. As a matter of fact, he just left."

"So, spill the beans. What happened? What did y'all do?"

"Dang, you sound like the police. Am I being interrogated? You know a girl doesn't kiss and tell."

"What?" Eden could hear Anya clapping. "I'm so excited."

"Excited about what, Anya?"

"You just said kiss and tell, that means you two kissed."

Eden screamed, "Yesssss. And, girl, I forgot how good that man could kiss. He had a sistah about to act crazy up in here, but he stopped because he's a doggone gentleman."

Anya started laughing. "Hey, twenty years have passed, things have changed. It's okay for you to take the lead."

Eden shook her head, even though Anya couldn't see her. "I can't end up dating Kingsley; we're not on the same level."

"Oh boy, here we go," Anya said. "Let's talk about this later over dinner and drinks."

Over the next couple of weeks, Kingsley came by and picked up Eden for lunch and walks in the park. They went to the mall, went sightseeing and talked about future business ideas. Eden tried her best not to get any closer to Kingsley because of their economic disparity but wondered if she was making a mistake. Kingsley was the kind of guy that you could take home to your family. It wasn't like he was too perfect. He had his faults, and he had been very transparent in sharing those with her. She reciprocated but didn't share that she wanted someone on the same economic level as she. Eden felt like today was the day to be honest.

"Hey, lady, what's going on in that head of yours? You are here and yet you're a million miles away."

"Kingsley, I have had a great time with you over this last month, but I don't know what we're doing here. What is all of this?"

"Eden, first off, I never thought I would see you or Anya ever again after we lost touch, so right now I am just enjoying the moment. I love your company and I love spending time with you. I'm hoping you feel the same way."

"I am, but I tend to keep my heart guarded."

"Well, then whatever this is, we can take it slow." He reached over and kissed her gently, and Eden wanted to melt again.

"Will you take me by my store? I have a surprise for you."

They arrived at the store, and Ashley and a couple of the other ladies were happy to see her. Eden introduced Kingsley to her staff, and the ladies all smiled.

"Kingsley, to thank you for saving my life, I want to have a couple of tailored suits made for you."

"No, Eden, you don't have to do that."

"I know I don't have to, but please, let me do this for you. Sit down with my tailor and tell him exactly what you want, and I don't want any mouthing off from you. Once your suits are done, you can come in and try them on and get some accessories to go with it. I'm thinking a great tie, cufflinks, socks and shoes would do the job."

"Eden, no, that's too much."

"Shush, it's the least I can do."

Kingsley relented and sat down with the tailor. While he was getting measured, Ashley and the staff kept smiling at Eden.

"What are you ladies smiling about?"

"Oh nothing. We're just wondering who in the world that fine man is you brought in here." Ashley said.

Eden rolled her eyes. "He's an old friend, and actually, he's the one that saved my life."

"Hmmmm," Ashley clicked her nails on the counter top. "So, are you two an item?"

"No, we're not an item. He has just been taking me around since the doctor hasn't released me to drive yet."

"Hmmmmm," Ashely continued clicking her nails on the counter top. "Well, just to let you know, Mr. UPS has been back asking about you."

"Has he now? Well, I'm still not interested."

"I can see why, especially with Mr. Kingsley."

"Ladies, it's nothing like that."

"Hmmmm," Ashley said again.

Ashley can't seem to find her words today. "You ladies know my rules on dating."

"Yes, we do. But some rules are made to be broken." Ashley said as the others nodded.

Eden shook her head. "Lawd, you all are as bad as Anya." They all laughed.

Eden returned to work two weeks later, and her tailor informed her that Kingsley's suits were ready. She buzzed him and told him to come over and try them on and pick out his accessories.

"Hey, beautiful ladies, how are you all today?"

"Fine, Mr. Kingsley," Ashley said as the other sales clerks smiled.

Kingsley cleared his throat. "Uh, is Eden in?"

"Yes, she's in her office, let me take you to her." Ashley said.

Eden heard the knock on her door as she was finishing up a call and motioned for them to enter. She hung up the phone and went around her desk to hug Kingsley.

"So, are you ready to get suited and booted?"

"Sure, if that's what you want." He looked around her office. "I'm loving this set up in your office. It's so eclectic."

"Glad you like it." She grabbed his hand. "Come on, let's go try your suits on."

"Okay, okay, I'm going."

Kingsley walked out of the dressing room, and Eden swore that her heart stopped. "Oh my," was all she could say. Kingsley looked so good in that suit and tie. The socks, shoes and cufflinks brought the whole ensemble together.

He modeled for her. "What do you think, Eden?"

"I think you can only wear that suit when you're with me."

Kingsley looked at her. "What did you just say?"

She rubbed the back of her neck. "I mean, it looks great on you. Everything matches perfectly." She shooed him back toward the dressing room. "Let's see the other one." Eden grabbed a bottle of water while she waited. "I can't wait to see what this next suit looks like."

Kingsley emerged again, and Eden's mouth dropped. The man looked like he belonged on a runway. He was already tall and thin, the suit was just that extra oomph.

"Wow, Kingsley, you clean up really well."

"I know I do, girl, you just never noticed."

"Well, I will be in my office when you finish. Have Pierre box up everything for you and just meet me back in my office."

Kingsley knocked on Eden's office door, and she yelled for him to come in.

"Looks like your staff has gone for the day, and Pierre said to tell you he was leaving." Eden stood. "Let me go make sure they locked up." She walked back into her office and sashayed over to him, leaning in close. She kissed him, and he kissed her back passionately.

Before they knew it, they were making love on the Italian leather sofa in Eden's office. They reassembled themselves and laughed.

"Oh my, we just acted like two hot teenagers," Eden said.

"Do you regret what just happened?"

"No."

"Me either."

That night on the sofa led to many other dates and romantic weekends that year. She was soon helping with his business and discovered Kingsley was doing pretty well for himself. He also helped her with her limo and real estate business. Eden had changed her mind about the financial situation and realized that she just wanted someone to love her and grow with her.

One weekend while jogging in Centennial Park, they happened to stop at the same spot where Eden had her appendicitis attack.

"Flashback?" Kingsley asked.

"Kinda sorta. Just think, this time last year, I was passed out on the ground and you found me and walked into my hospital room." When Kingsley didn't say anything, she turned around.

Kingsley was on one knee, looking up at her. "Yea, and next year I want you to be Mrs. Kingsley Smith. Eden, will you marry me?"

Eden had learned that love can come in all kinds of packages, and it could even walk back into your life after you missed out on it the first time. She was going to make sure they didn't lose each other again.

"Yes, yes, yes," she screamed.

Kingsley stood and the two shared a passionate kiss. Two unlikely companions had come full circle, back to the place where love walked in.

About the Author

Alicia Fleming has always had a passion for reading and writing. Growing up in Mt. Juliet, Tennessee – a suburb twenty minutes outside of Nashville, Alicia enjoys the solitude that comes with reading and writing. Graduating from Middle Tennessee State University (MTSU) years ago with a Bachelor of Science degree in Public Relations, Alicia realized her passion for writing. She wants to make an impact on people through her writing, travels and photography. She wants her gift to be used to bless others in a positive way and to encourage people. When she is not spending time with her husband, David and adult daughter, Megan, Alicia enjoys reading, writing, traveling and just having fun with family and friends.

Visit her online at aliciaclemmonsfleming.com

Love Walked In

The Gala Replacement
T.A. Beasley

Mia Stone slid her coffee cup off the kitchen counter and made her way to the front porch. Mia loved the quiet hum of her neighborhood. She slid deeper into the plush cushion of the rattan armchair and rested her feet on the ottoman, enjoying the wisps of steam curling over the rim of her coffee mug. Her journal and pencil rested on the small table beside her. Mrs. Branson, her elderly neighbor to the left would be joining her shortly for their daily cup of java. The feisty older woman had been the first to greet Mia when she moved into her ranch style home a year ago, and now after their morning routine of Mia's journaling and Mrs. Branson's bible reading, the gesture continued. Thinking of her neighbor, Mia smiled and settled into writing her thoughts, feelings and to do list. She always started with what she was grateful for and then followed with her affirmations for the day.

Thirty minutes later, the last line in her journal was complete. Mia looked at her watch. "Hmm, Mrs. Branson is usually here by now. She glanced across her yard, a moving truck was backing up to Ms. Branson's house. *She's not moving, is she?* Mia placed her journal on the table, grabbed her cup and went to the end of the porch. A handsome man was slinging a chair over his shoulder.

He swung his head full of dreadlocked hair as he exited the house. Mia watched the dark-skinned muscular body reach back to lift a second chair with ease. Fully engrossed in the man's movements, she leaned a little too far and like a slow motion camera outtake, Mia saw Ms. Branson dispatch the man to her assistance, then she felt huge hands steady her before she stumbled. Embarrassed, Mia smiled sheepishly.

The man stepped back. "Ma'am, your phone is ringing."

Mesmerized by the deep baritone voice swaying across her ears, Mia didn't move.

The muscular man moved towards her and pointed at her small table. "Ma'am, your phone."

Mia followed his hand. "Ohhhh, excuse me." She looked back over her shoulder. "Thanks for your help," she said before grabbing her phone and going inside.

"Hello."

"Hello, Mia, it's your mother."

She looked out the window at her neighbor's house. "Hi, Mom."

"Darling, I have the perfect man for you to meet."

Ugh, not again. Mia wiped her hand over her face. *My mom would marry me off to a stranger if she could.* She knew her mom just wanted to remind her about the charity ball happening in three weeks. "Mom, I don't need you to find me a date."

"Honey, listen to me. This man is perfect for you. His name is Calvin Cox, and he owns two skate rinks, two arcades and a laser tag business. Calvin can take care of you."

"Mom, seriously?"

"Well, I need grandbabies before the good Lord takes me home."

Mia fisted her hair and rushed her response without thinking. "Mom, I don't need you to find me a date. I already have one." She hated lying to her mother.

"Oh! This is wonderful news, Mia. What is his name and what does he do for a living?" Mia could hear her mother clapping her hands and knew she was probably smiling from ear to ear.

"I have to go, Mom, but you'll meet him at the ball." Mia hung up the phone and went to check on her neighbor.

Mia realized her situation was not ideal. She didn't have a date and she only had three weeks to find one and educate him on Mia 101. If she was going to pull this off, she needed Tabitha. Mia picked up the phone. After three rings, the voicemail picked up. "Hey, Tabby, it's me, Mia. I have this life or death situation, and I need your help as soon as possible." She knew Tabitha would probably laugh, but Mia was desperate.

Mia had sworn off dating. A year ago, on the morning of their fourth anniversary, Mia let herself into Darius' house to surprise him with breakfast. She made her way to his bedroom with the breakfast tray and shouted, "Happy Anniversary!" But when she saw Darius still in bed and the expression on his face, the tray slipped out of her hand and crashed to the floor. Her thirty-nine year old boyfriend lay dead from a brain aneurysm.

Remembering that morning always brought tears to her eyes, and Mia hadn't dated because she didn't want to disrespect his memory. But, if she walked into that ball without a date, she knew her mother would pawn her off on Calvin, the skating rink king. Mia shook her head and opened her email. She would get some work done while waiting for Tabitha to call back. As a virtual assistant for filmmakers, her home business always had a steady amount of tasks.

Mia passed the day completing several projects and emailing promo graphics to a client. After work, she grabbed a book to read and settled on the couch to relax. A knock at her door startled her. She dogeared the page and went to see who was there. From the peephole, Tabitha grinned holding up a bag of Munchos and a bottle of Mountain Dew.

Mia chuckled and opened the door. "Tabs, I knew you would come through."

Smiling, Tabitha made her way to the kitchen and smiled. "Girl, you know I had to come with my strategy planning kit. I just need a cup and some ice."

Mia rolled her eyes. "Could you hurry please? I need your help with Operation: Find a Fake Charity Ball Date."

Tabitha busted out laughing, spraying drink across the counter. "Is that what this life and death situation is about?" She wiped her face with a paper towel and pulled another one off the roll to clean the counter. "Girl, I thought someone was after you and we had to plan your escape."

"Really, Tabs? You always want to go to the dark side."

Tabitha took her snacks to the dining room table. "So tell me how I can help?"

Mia grabbed a glass of water before joining her friend at the table. She recounted the conversation with her mother and told her friend about the man at her neighbor's house and how he saved her from falling off the porch. Mia sighed. "I'm pretty sure he's the reason the fake date idea came spewing out when Mother called."

Tabitha looked at her. "Well, let's just ask him."

Mia shook her head. "I can't. I don't know his name. All I know is he works at a furniture company."

"My point exactly. You know the name of the furniture company. Maybe your neighbor knows his name."

"She might, but I can't ask her. It would be too obvious."

Tabitha shrugged. "Welp, back to the drawing board then. Good thing I never leave home without these." She placed two small address books on the table. "And no, it's not what you think. These are filled with contact info for colleagues I've worked with or have done business with."

Mia laughed. "I was concerned for a moment."

Tabitha shook her head. "Get your mind out of the gutter. I'm going to the living room to make some calls on your behalf."

"And I appreciate it."

Tabitha looked over her shoulder. "Totally off subject, but I almost forgot to tell you, Madison will be calling you to babysit Lulu while she is out of town next week."

Mia opened her laptop to check her schedule. "Why can't you watch her?"

"I watched her two months ago when Madison was in New York for that fashion show."

Mia, Tabitha and Madison met in college and became friends after working on a marketing project together. Whenever Madison, an up and coming fashion designer, goes out of town, she refuses to leave her pug, Lulu in doggy daycares for fear that Lulu will catch some doggy disease, so Mia and Tabitha take turns babysitting. "Well, I guess it's my turn, but I'll wait till she calls me."

After an hour of making phone calls with no luck, they decide to call it quits. "Don't worry," Tabitha said to Mia,

"We'll find you a date for the ball. I'm sure someone will return my call."

Mia shook her head. "I have faith. I'm not worried."

Mia hugged her friend goodbye and watched as Tabitha made her way to her car.

Later that evening as Mia prepared for bed, Tabitha called. "Guess what?"

"I'm sure you're going to tell me."

Tabitha laughed. "I found you a date."

"Yes!" Mia spun around, and then stopped her happy dance. "Wait, who is it?"

"Hear me out since it's last minute."

"Oh no, who is it, Tabs?"

"Parker."

"Are you kidding me right now?"

"I slave to find you a fake charity ball date and this is how you react?"

"I'm sorry, but Parker. You know he gets on my nerves."

Parker graduated a year before them. He had asked Mia out on a date several times, but she would never go. It didn't help that his mother owned one of Mia's favorite clothing stores, and he always seemed to be watching the store for his mother when Mia and Tabitha were there shopping.

"I know, but he is the only one in my book who is available that weekend." Tabitha explained.

Mia switched the phone to the opposite shoulder. "I need to let this settle in." If she didn't go with Parker, her mother would be marrying her off to Calvin by the end of the charity ball. "Okay, I'll deal with it."

"Good. You're meeting him at the dog park next week."

"Why the dog park?"

"First, because you'll have Lulu. And second, you know you don't want Parker knowing where you live. I know I don't."

"You make a good point. I owe you one."

"Yes, you do. And, look at it this way, he already knows everything about you. This will be easy for him to pull off."

"Tabs, he does know this is a fake date, right? I don't want him getting any ideas."

"Mia, I've made it very clear to him. Besides, I'll be there just in case he tries anything."

"Thanks, Tabs. You're a lifesaver."

"No problem. I got your back. I'll talk to you later."

"Lulu, slow down. We're almost there." Mia laughed. Madison's pug was walking as fast as her little legs could carry her. They rounded the last corner to the park, and Mia stopped short, yanking Lulu's lash. The guy who had moved Mrs. Branson's furniture was leaving the park with a chocolate lab. Mia bent to tie her shoe, placing some distance between his exit and her entrance.

When she finally entered the dog park, she removed Lulu's leash. "Go play, girl." After giving Lulu a rub on her back, she located her fake date. "Hello, Parker. I didn't know you liked animals."

"You wouldn't since you've never given us a chance."

Mia put the leash in her pocket and moved to the left of the fence where Parker leaned. "Don't rehash the past. We are not here for that."

"Tabitha was very clear about what we're here for. Why don't you tell me about this gala?"

Mia gritted her teeth. "At the *charity ball*, we will have to convince my mother that we've been dating for a while."

"Is there any additional information about you I need to know?"

Mia placed her hands on her hip. "Why would you ask that? What do you already know about me?"

Parker chuckled. "I know you run a successful virtual assistant business. Your favorite color is teal, favorite ice cream is butter pecan with cherry Pepsi poured over it. You love reading mysteries and thrillers and binge watching the Investigative Discovery channel."

Mia's mouth hung open.

"How am I doing so far? I also know you lost a fiancé, and your mother has been trying to marry you off since college because she wants grandchildren." Parker bent down to pet his dog who had wandered over. He handed him a treat.

"What's his name?" Mia let the dog smell her hand.

"Luke." Parker smiled.

"Hello, Luke." Mia tussled the dog's hair as he licked her other hand before prancing off to the other dogs.

Parker and Mia continued their conversation about the charity ball. She told him to wear a tux or a nice black suit to complement her teal gown, and then discussed where they should meet. Parker seemed amiable to all of Mia's instructions. She almost reached out to touch his arm, but wanted to be certain he didn't get any mixed signals. She clasped her hands together. "Parker, I just want you to know, I do appreciate you helping me."

Parker nodded and whistled for Luke. "It's no problem, Mia. I'll see you next Saturday." He leashed his dog and shook Mia's hand before walking away.

Mia looked around for Lulu and found her by a tree with another dog. "C'mon, Lulu. Let's head home."

The day before the gala, the event planner's assistant became ill and couldn't make it, so Mia was helping her mother with last-minute decorations. Crystal tapestry hung from the ceiling of the event hall while blue, gray and black colored décor adorned the space. Mia placed a runner on the table. "Mother, do you want the donation cards on the plate or table tented in front of the plate?"

"You know, that is a thought. Let me see both." Her mother watched as Mia fixed a table setting displaying both ideas. She leaned her head to the side. "Hmm, I'll go with on the plate."

After getting everything in place, Mia's mom took her to lunch at Mama Corolla's Italian restaurant, one of her favorite places. Mia loved the homemade lasagna and bread, especially the oil they served with the bread. "Wow, Mom! How did you get a table at Mama Corolla's?"

Her mother smiled. "You have to know the right people, darling."

Mia placed her clutch on the table and took her seat. "Well, I love that you know the right people. Thanks for taking me to lunch."

"You are welcome, dear."

Mia stared at her mother. "Why are we really here, Mom? Is there something wrong with Dad?"

"Your father? Oh no. It's not that. I just wanted to spend time with you."

"Mom, you never just want to spend time with me." Mia used air quotes to emphasize her mom's words and leaned back in her chair. "Tell me what's going on."

"Well, your father invited the Tuckers to the charity ball, and I just didn't want you to be caught off guard or… uncomfortable."

"Why would he do that? He knows I'm bringing a date." Mia placed her hand on her temple, trying to soothe the headache that was forming. "I mean I haven't spoken to them since Darius' funeral."

"His little sister is up for one of the scholarships this year, and your father wanted them there to accept if she wins."

"Or is it that Dad is going to make sure she wins and make things more awkward for me?" Mia shook her head. "And, wouldn't she be in the category he's making me present? This is so wrong."

"It's not that bad, honey. It will go by fast. Besides, your handsome man will be there to take your mind off things. He is still coming, right?"

Mia ignored her mother's question, wondering to herself, *What else can happened to me?*

Mia arrived early to the charity ball at her father's request. After going over her presentation with him and assuring him she had everything under control, Mia's mother introduced her to two of the other speakers for the evening who happened to be civic leaders. Mia made small talk, but her attention kept returning to the door. She was waiting for Parker to arrive. *I'm going to kill him if he is late.* Mia smiled as her mother went on and on. After finding an appropriate moment to excuse herself, she walked away looking in her clutch for her phone. Exasperated, she closed her handbag. "Ugh, I left my phone in the car."

Tabitha put the last touches on her makeup and grabbed her purse. She was about to walk out the door when her cell phone rang. "Hello."

"Thank God I was finally able to reach one of you."

"Who is this?" She stopped midstride.

"It's me, Parker. I have been trying to reach Mia, but she isn't answering her phone."

Tabitha resumed her pace and opened her car. "Are you okay? You sound weird."

"I'm afraid I have some bad news, Tab. I'm at the hospital. I tripped over my dog coming down the stairs and broke my leg. The doctor says I'll need a cast. Please tell Mia I'm sorry."

"You have got to be kidding me, Parker."

"I'm dead serious, Tabs. I can't make it tonight. Be sure to tell Mia I'm sorry, okay?"

Tabitha adjusted her steering wheel. "You're serious, aren't you? I'm sorry about your leg, even though I want to kill you right now."

"I know. This could not have happened at a worse time."

"Take care of your leg, Parker. I'll find a way to break this to Mia. No pun intended."

"None taken. The nurse is here, so I need to go. Sorry again, Tab."

Tabitha disconnected and headed to Mia's house. She pulled up to her friend's house and rang the doorbell. When Mia didn't answer, she pounded on the door. Tabitha saw Mia's neighbor in her peripheral and ran to catch her. "Mrs. Branson! Mrs. Branson!"

"Slow down, child, before you fall."

"Hi, I'm Tabitha. I'm a friend of Mia, your neighbor." She tried to catch her breath.

"I know who you are, dear. This here is my grandson, Marquel." Mrs. Branson pointed in the direction of the handsome man assisting her into the car.

"Hello, Marquel, nice to meet you." Tabitha smiled, wondering if this was the same guy with dreads, muscular arms and the strength of Samson that Mia had seen at her neighbors last week.

"Baby, what can I help you with?" Mrs. Branson asked.

Tabitha shook her head. "I'm sorry. I was looking for Mia. Have you seen her? I knocked but there was no answer."

"She left early for the ball. We're headed there now. My grandson is attending with me in place of his father this year."

"Oh no! She's already there?" Tabitha gripped her head.

"What has you all rattled? Can we help you with something?" Marquel's deep voice cascaded over Tabitha.

Tabitha looked up. "Wow," she said before she could catch herself. "You know, there is something you can help me with, Marquel, if Mrs. Branson doesn't mind."

Mia's neighbor nodded her head as Tabitha shared about Mia and her mother. "I know the Stones, dear, and I know a lot of things about Mia. Now that Marquel has agreed to your favor, I will handle it from here." Mrs. Branson informed Tabitha. "We will see you there."

"Thank you both. You're a lifesaver."

Despite her mother introducing her to every eligible bachelor she could find, Mia was still watching the door for Parker. She looked up from her drink and saw Tabs waving at her.

"How come you didn't tell me you were coming early?" Tabitha made her way over to Mia. "I went by your house since Parker couldn't get ahold of you."

"Why was Parker trying to get ahold of me? He is supposed to be here already."

"Yeah, about that, he broke his leg and won't be able to make it."

"No, this can't happen, not tonight." Mia dropped into a chair. "My life is ruined. I can't marry the skate rink king."

"Did you think I would leave you hanging? You know Tabs always has a backup plan." She grabbed Mia's drink and took a sip. "Sprite. Really, Mia? We need a drink drink."

"What are you talking about? My night is about to go downhill and you're worried about what I'm drinking."

Tabitha grasped Mia's shoulders and lifted her from the chair. She looked over at the door and whispered in Mia's ear. "Calm down, drama queen, and go meet your date."

Mia followed Tabs' eyes to the door. The furniture guy with the dreads walked in and over to her. He pulled her in an embrace, resting his lips at the nape of her ear. "My name is Marquel and your friend said you needed help. I'm here for you so just go with it."

Marquel drew Mia into a slow dance, and Mia's eyes landed on her mother who had stopped talking and turned to watch her daughter. From the middle of the floor, Mia looked over at Tabitha and mouthed, "Thank you."

The couple continued dancing as Ed Sheeran's *Thinking Out Loud* played over the speaker. Mia felt like she was in heaven as they swayed back and forth, their bodies in perfect sync to the lyrics. Marquel twirled her around as the song came to an end. She looked up at him and smiled. "I think I've found love right where I am."

He leaned towards her and smiled. Their lips met as Mia reached up towards him. A roar of applause filled the room, bringing Mia back to reality and the ball. They made their way to her table. "How did Tabs rope you into this?"

"All cards on the table? It wasn't all her. My grandmother is your next door neighbor, and I had asked her about you. I guess she overheard you and Tabitha talking about your fake date or something, so I asked if I could come with her tonight to see you."

"That is where I come in." Tabitha bulldozed into the conversation. "I asked him to step into Parker's place, and he agreed. Now you two can be together, for real together not fake wise."

"We get it, Tabs. Now, can we talk alone? Thanks!" Mia shooed her friend off and turned back to Marquel. "Sorry, sometimes she has no filter."

"I can see that." Marquel laughed.

Mia looked over Marquel's shoulder. "My mother is making her way over here to analyze you. Is there anything I need to know besides you are in the furniture business? I'm sure you have some questions about me."

He shook his head. "No, your friend and my grandmother filled me in on all things Mia, so I'm covered. But I will tell you, I'm glad I finally got to meet you."

"You don't understand how much it means to me that you were the one to walk through that door." She gave him a side eye. "We'll discuss the dance floor kiss later." The two shared a laugh as Mia's mother approached.

"Let the questions begin," Marquel said. He lifted their entwined hands and gently kissed the back of Mia's hand. "I, too, am glad that I walked in."

About the Author

T. A. Beasley is an author, blogger and book reviewer who loves all things literary. Her love for books prompted her to start *Authors & Readers Book Corner*, a blog that supports authors by sharing their books with readers. She is the author of *It Happened To Me* and founder of LaBrice Books. Beasley resides in Indianapolis, Indiana, with her husband.

Visit her online at tabeasley.weebly.com

Love Walked In

When the Past Comes Calling
Jeanette Hill

Ruth was going a bit stir crazy. Three years had passed since Martin's illness took him from her just as they were starting to enjoy retirement. And while she had no financial worries, nothing – not time, not money or children could fill the void. Ruth felt conflicted. She was grateful for Davis and Allison. When Davis's job transferred him back to Ruth's hometown, her son and daughter-in-law insisted she move in with them, but she needed to get out of the house and do something...with people her age. She needed a life and people her own age to help her enjoy it, that's how Ruth found herself back in her old neighborhood.

Most of the houses in her old neighborhood had been replaced with condos and boutique businesses with names like *The Juicery* and *Brittani's Yoga Palace.*

She pulled into what used to be *Miller's Grocery and Produce Store,* but the newly remodeled, contemporary building told her it was no longer a mom and pop grocery. She hated spending so much time reading labels. Diabetes was taking away her last guilty pleasure— eating. She stopped when she thought she heard someone calling her name.

"Ruth?" It was more of a question than a greeting. A tall, dark skinned man with salt and pepper hair gave her a questioning look. "Ruth Sullivan?

155

She squinted as he came closer. "Clyde! Clyde Anderson?" More than forty years had passed since she'd seen Clyde, but that Anderson walk was unmistakable. All of the Anderson boys had bowed legs and walked with a little swagger. When he neared, those deep dimples confirmed it was him.

"Ruth! I haven't seen you in..." They hugged in that familiar way old friends did and stepped back, eyeing each other to see what had changed and what had not. "Wow, you still look good."

"So do you!"

"A little less hair and what's left is gray, but I can't complain." Clyde took off his cap and rubbed his head.

She laughed. "Let's not talk about gray hair, okay?"

"I haven't seen you around here before."

She shook her head. "After my husband died, I moved in with my son and his family in Spring Hills."

"I'm sorry to hear that. I lost my Deborah two years ago. Cancer."

Nodding, Ruth watched the memory of his loss make its way onto his face. "Do you have any children?"

Clyde laughed. "Six. Five boys and one daughter, just like my parents. So did three of my boys, Josh, Michael and Benjamin. Paul chickened out and didn't have any. Paulette my only girl, had twins and stopped. She was scared that since she and Paul were twins, she didn't want to start a new tradition. How about you, just the one?"

Ruth shook her head. "We went the traditional route. A boy and a girl, Davis and Regina. Davis's job transferred him here several years ago, that's how I got back here. Regina settled in Kansas City, she travels a lot for work. Your kids live around here?"

"Josh, Benjamin and Paulette live here. Michael lives in Dallas with his family. Steve is making a career of the military, they're in Hawaii now, and Paul is in the tech field. He lives in Atlanta."

"I bet holidays were quite an event at your house."

"Still are. Six kids, thirteen grandchildren, two great grands and one on the way! Around here, politicians don't go to churches, they come to our house. By the way, what church does your family attend? We're still at Macedonia."

"We attend a non-denominational church. It's mostly white but—"

"Heaven isn't segregated as long as Jesus is there." Clyde laughed. "Hey, several of us from high school get together every third Saturday for breakfast at Mabel's. Why don't you join us next Saturday? You know most of them: James Harris, Scott Bell, and Trudie Norris?"

"Of course, I do. Scott and Trudie tore up that skating rink. They're still together?"

Clyde rolled his eyes, "They married right after graduation. Got divorced. Remarried. Divorced again. Married other people. Got divorced. Now, they're headed to the altar again."

"Are you kidding?"

"We don't pay attention anymore. James Harris and Arlene are still together. Sonny and... Look, just come to breakfast, you can catch up then. What do you say?"

With more confidence than she felt, she said, "Sounds like fun, Clyde. I'd love to."

"We meet at Mabel's at nine o'clock."

"Mabel's is still open? With all the changes around here, I was sure it had been a casualty."

"Her granddaughter, Gwen runs it now. She's Mabel all over again," he laughed. "But they are still hanging on. Look, give me your number and email. I'll send you the information about breakfast. Are you on Facebook? We have a private group on there."

"I don't know much about social media." Ruth gave him her information.

He put it in his wallet. "I'll send you the information when I get home. It was good to see you, Ruth." He hugged her again.

Ruth checked her email as soon as she got home and Clyde's email was there. She asked her grandson, Martin to tutor her on Facebook.

"Facebook? You've never had an interest in social media before, Mother." Her request surprised Davis.

"I ran into an old schoolmate at the grocery store today. Our old high school group has a Facebook page, and they meet once a month for breakfast. He invited me to attend."

Allison hugged Ruth. "I think it's great that you are meeting new 'old' friends."

"Martin, make sure you show your grandmother the safety features on Facebook. I don't want her getting her identity stolen. And, Mother, be careful. Don't give out too much information, okay?"

Clyde called her just as Martin finished setting up her Facebook account. "Did I catch you at a bad time? I'm wanted to make sure you got my email and understood the instructions for accessing our group."

She hadn't noticed how deep his voice was while they were talking in the store.

"Martin just finished setting it up. He says someone will have to give me access to it."

"Don't worry about that. I am one of the administrators."

Martin gave her a thumbs up to let her know he was finished. "Grandma, tell him you just sent a request to join." He kissed her and left her in front of the computer.

"Martin says that he sent a request—"

"I've already approved it. You'll see pictures going back to high school."

She scrolled through the photos. "Oh my goodness, there's a picture of our cheerleading squad. Goodness! Can something be done to that photo to take some that weight off of me?"

"What are you talking about? You looked fine. Half the guys on the team were trying to get at you."

"Yeah, right. Get to me to do their math homework."

"See? Brains and beauty."

Remembering the crush she had on Clyde in high school, she felt silly getting all worked up about a compliment. Clyde and Ruth reminisced about special times growing up in the neighborhood.

They said their goodnights, and Ruth found she was looking forward to Saturday's brunch. A slight noise startled her. "Did you need something, Davis?"

"You seem excited about this breakfast. Have a good time, but remember, people change over time."

"I know, Davis. It's only brunch. I'll be fine, really."

Davis bent down and kissed her good night.

Ruth was up early Saturday morning going through her closet. *It's a breakfast, Ruth, not a job interview. Just pick something.* She decided on a dark blue pantsuit, a floral print blouse and low heels. She triple checked herself in the mirror before leaving her room.

Davis offered to drop her off, but the last thing she wanted her old high school friends to think was that she couldn't get around on her own. Mabel's parking lot was almost full by the time she arrived. As she stepped inside the restaurant the smell of food and the sound of boisterous chatter met her. Clyde was on his way to greet her.

"I'm so glad you made it." He led her to a side room of the restaurant where she recognized some familiar and not so familiar faces.

"Hey, everybody. You remember Ruth Sullivan...Willis? She was in our class, well, my class. "And, if you are like me, you are horrible with names, so let's go around the table and introduce ourselves. Start down at the end with Sam."

There was no mistaking the man with his big eyes and infectious smile, wearing a polo shirt a size too small, Sam Little the class clown.

"How could she forget me? I got ten detentions trying to make her laugh." His wide grin caused his eyes to disappear. "And, I know you recognize Trudie with all those freckles on her face."

"Chile, I tried to bleach them for twenty years until I just gave up!" Trudie laughed.

Two waitresses came to take their drink orders. After they left, the roll call started again. The only person she didn't remember was the woman sitting across from her. Try as she might, she couldn't place her, but Clyde came to her rescue.

"You won't remember Margie. She moved to the area right after graduation. I think you had left by then. She married Tony Cook, and we adopted her into our class."

"I remember Tony." She looked around the table. "Is he joining us today?"

The table became silent. Ruth immediately knew something was wrong.

"Tony passed several months ago," Margie said.

"I'm so sorry," Ruth told her. "I'm familiar with the pain of losing a spouse as well."

Margie offered a weak smile, and Clyde passed Ruth a menu. "We were just getting ready to get in line. We usually get the buffet but there are other options."

Ruth decided to follow the crowd. The buffet table was adorned with colorful floral arrangements. The food looked and smelled delicious. There were cheese grits, sausage, bacon, ham, scrambled eggs, fried potatoes with peppers and onions, fresh fruit and homemade biscuits. She decided she'd get back on her health regimen tomorrow.

Margie suddenly excused herself with Clyde close behind her. He returned to the table a few moments later explaining she had to leave. At the end of breakfast, Ruth exchanged contact information with everyone at the table before Clyde walked her out. "Well, did you enjoy yourself? As you can see, we haven't changed that much besides a little gray hair, a few more pounds...and moving a little slower.

Ruth laughed. Since Martin's death, Ruth hadn't felt as though she fit in anywhere. "I did enjoy myself. Thanks for inviting me."

"Hopefully, you won't make this your last time joining us. "

"I won't," she smiled, "but, I should be on my way."

"I'll talk to you soon, Ruth. Be safe."

To her surprise, Allison was cooking lunch. To be more accurate, she was putting together the contents from one of those home delivery meal services. It looked like some kind of chicken pasta dish.

Allison glanced over her shoulder. "It must be pouring out there."

"It is, started just as I left the restaurant. I hate driving in rain." Ruth shed her wet coat. "Is that pasta salad for lunch or dinner?"

"Neither, Celeste Cummings is hosting our book club meeting today and everyone is bringing some type of salad." She looked at her watch. "I better get dressed. I'm late. Davis and Martin went to a movie. They're planning to eat out, so you won't have to cook."

The house was so quiet after Allison left that Ruth put on some music. She'd just started relaxing when her cell phone rang.

"Yes?"

"Hey, I was just calling to make sure you made it home okay."

Ruth smiled. She hadn't expected to hear from Clyde.

"How thoughtful of you. I did, but I probably gave some people road rage."

"Better for you to be safe. I hear music. You having a party?"

Ruth turned down the music.

"I'm really glad you joined us today. Can't believe so much time has passed. Anyway, I won't hold you. Bye."

The front door opened, and Davis and Martin entered chatting excitedly.

"Well, it seems like you two enjoyed the movie. What did you see?" Ruth asked.

Martin was almost jumping up and down. "We didn't go to the movies. We went to a video game exhibit. It was lit!"

Ruth smiled. She wasn't quite sure what lit meant but given Martin's exuberance, it was something good.

Clyde and Ruth talked almost daily for the next few weeks. After church, one Sunday, Ruth thought about inviting Clyde over. Instead, she went on Facebook to see if he might be on there. Her phone rang.

"Hello," Clyde said. "How are you?"

"Hey, Clyde. I'm good, thanks."

"We had a full day at church today. It was the usher's annual."

"I saw the photos Trudie posted on Facebook."

"They served a big dinner after three o'clock service, so nobody had to cook. I cooked anyway. I usually do on Sundays."

"So you cook, huh? What's your signature dish?"

"I can cook most things, but I do a pretty good lasagna. Granny taught all of us boys how to cook. She didn't want some good *cooking* woman to lure any of her boys away." He laughed. "We were teenagers. The last thing on our minds was whether or not a girl could cook."

"She was giving you life skills. She knew about teenage boys."

"I think I am going to take a ride. What are you doing? I can pick you up and we can get some ice cream or something."

"Well...ah, okay. Sure."

"Great. I'll pick you up in about forty-five minutes."

Ruth put on a short-sleeved print maxi dress. *It's not a date,* she told herself as she sat in the living room, peeking out the window every few minutes.

A few moments later, the doorbell rang. Before Ruth could stand, Davis was at the door.

Clyde was dressed in a short-sleeved shirt and creased jeans. He introduced himself and gave Davis a firm handshake. He smiled when he spotted Ruth standing just behind her son. "It's nice to meet you. Your mother speaks of you often."

Davis asked him to have a seat. Ruth knew Clyde would oblige. They came from an era where it was considered impolite to rush in and out of someone's home. Soon, Clyde suggested they get going. She hadn't noticed his late model dark blue Lincoln MKX at Mabel's Place. Davis stood in the door waving goodbye as they pulled out of the driveway.

"I hope you weren't embarrassed with Davis asking you so many questions."

"Not at all. If it was me, I probably would have made copies my driver's license."

They rode around for about an hour, then stopped at an ice cream truck. Clyde got the vanilla/chocolate swirl dish and Ruth chose strawberry. They sat on a nearby bench.

"Do you remember the ice cream stand on Lennox where we all went to on Saturday afternoons?" Clyde asked.

Ruth chuckled. "Yes. All the girls use to 'walk' to that ice cream stand to meet boys."

"Did you ever think our lives would turn out like this? I mean being alone."

Ruth knew the life cycle would touch her just like it touched everybody else. "We never talked about life without the other... like we'd be young forever."

Clyde nodded in agreement. "You know what's funny? I know the mirror can't lie, but even with the aches, pains and creaking joints, I don't feel any different inside," he laughed. "Until a pretty young girl with a big smile looks at me and I push my shoulders back and pull my stomach in, then she tells me that I remind her of her favorite uncle."

"Well, women my age get, 'It's the old lady from down the street.'"

"You're not anybody's old lady. Come on, it's getting dark." He pulled her up, and they stood close for a brief second before walking to the car. Along the way, their hands touched and stayed together.

When they reached her house, Clyde walked her to the door.

Ruth turned. "Thank you, Clyde. I had a nice time."

Clyde leaned in and kissed her lightly on the lips. "Good night, Ruth."

"Did you have a good time?" Davis was sitting in the living room.

Ruth nodded. As she got ready for bed, she thought about the drive, the ice cream, the walk, the talk...and the kiss.

The next week, Clyde asked Ruth to dinner. They decided to have dinner early Friday night so that she could get home before it was too late.

She remembered his one-story brick house with gray trim. There were miniature yellow roses on each side of the stairs and the walkway was edged with small hedges.

He greeted her with a peck on the cheek and took her coat. "You can put your purse on the table. Come on back to the kitchen. Can I get you something to drink? Water or tea? If you're inclined, I have an adult beverage."

"Water is fine." The kitchen was nicely remodeled and was large for a house this size. "You have a beautiful home. Dinner smells good. What is it?"

He laughed as he checked the oven. "We're having my world famous lasagna."

"Can I help with anything?"

Clyde maneuvered in the kitchen with ease. "You can grab the salad, dressing and iced tea from the fridge. Everything else is ready."

He placed the lasagna on the table. Ruth got the items from the fridge. Clyde poured the tea and then pulled out her chair. He blessed the food and passed the salad bowl to Ruth while he served the lasagna.

He had just started to eat when his doorbell rang. Frowning, he excused himself. Ruth couldn't see who it was from where she sat, but she could tell it was a woman. After a few minutes, Clyde came down the hall pulling Margie behind him. Visibly upset, she avoided eye contact with Ruth.

Clyde pulled her to the table, and Margie reluctantly sat. "Margie was in the neighborhood and stopped by. I asked her to stay for dinner. You don't mind do you, Ruth?"

Ruth gave Margie a smile that didn't quite make it to her eyes. "Of course not. Join us. There's plenty of food, and Clyde tells me he's a great cook." What did Clyde expect her to say? *This evening is about you and me, not a third wheel.* Ruth hated feeling that way, she knew all too well what it was like to be the odd person at dinner.

Clyde put some of the lasagna on Margie's plate, but she only picked at it. Clyde tried to carry the conversation with Ruth joining in where she could. After about twenty minutes, Margie excused herself and headed for the door. Clyde followed. Ruth decided to offer to help, but when she turned down the hallway, she saw Clyde and Margie in a tight embrace. Ruth stood there watching for a moment and then went back to the dining table.

Clyde returned to the table and asked Ruth if she wanted him to warm her food. Without any explanation, he started talking about the process for preparing the food as though Margie had never been there. True, they weren't in a committed relationship, but he had invited her to dinner, so she assumed... Her appetite was gone. She thanked him for dinner and made a hasty exit.

Ruth knew Clyde was watching from the porch. She had tears in eyes and didn't know why. She'd been sitting in her car for a few minutes when she saw Clyde coming out of the house. She quickly backed out of the driveway, leaving him standing at the bottom of the steps.

The image of Clyde and Margie stayed in her mind all the way home. She tried to rush past Allison without attracting attention, but Allison called after her. "You're back early. Did you have a nice dinner?"

Ruth nodded without turning.

"Did something happen?" Ruth shook her head as Allison looked at her look face. "Something *is* wrong. Davis!"

"Please! Don't. It's nothing. I'm going to take a hot shower and go to bed. Really, everything is fine." She rushed to her room, and this time, the tears didn't stay in her eyes.

She took Martin to practice the next afternoon but was still feeling some kind of way about last night's dinner. Clyde had called four times, but she ignored his calls, letting them go to voicemail. What was he going to say? Apologize for making her feel like some boy crazy, high school girl?

She did the laundry, rearranged the pantry, dusted, mopped and cooked dinner to keep her mind off of Clyde but it hadn't worked. Martin was going over his friend, Ethan's house after practice. *Why didn't she have any friends?* More time on her hands, at least the calls had stopped. She decided to read the community paper and saw that a new gardening group was starting in a few weeks, but the idea of spending her days with gray-haired women in sensible shoes and straw hats talking about grandchildren, recipes and rheumatism didn't appeal to her.

She checked her email before getting ready for bed. There were three emails from Clyde. Why she was so upset? What was wrong with her? She was still a good-looking woman. If she wanted a man, there were plenty of them. Okay, maybe not in her age bracket but still... It was such a depressing thought that she went to bed.

Strange, she'd spent the previous day avoiding his calls, and this morning she was upset because he stopped calling. She decided to go to Lowe's to look at plants, but when she opened her door, Clyde was standing there.

"So you are alive! After twelve phone calls, four emails and seven texts, I was getting worried."

"Clyde! What are you doing here?"

His face said she knew why he was there. "I think we need to talk."

Ruth stepped aside and let him in. He followed her into the living room. "Would you like something to drink?"

"What I'd like is an explanation. What's going on? You won't answer my calls. You ignore my emails and texts...."

Ruth scowled. How could he act like he didn't know what was wrong? "Clyde, I am... We both are too old to play games."

Clyde looked confused. Ruth waited for him to respond. When he didn't, she continued. "I know we haven't been together long. Okay, maybe together isn't the right word. But I thought we had the start of... I don't know, but I do know that I deserved better than being deceived."

"Deceived about what? What are you talking about? I thought were getting along fine. I enjoy your company and I thought you enjoyed mine. That's why I don't understand why you just dropped me. No explanation. No nothing."

"What I saw at dinner the other night was self-explanatory. So if I didn't need an explanation, neither should you."

"What do you think you saw?"

"I'm not a fool, Clyde. I saw you and Margie embracing in the hallway. Inviting her to join us for dinner. Kissing her—"

Clyde stood. "Ruth, I kissed her on the forehead. I invited her to join us because she was upset. It was her wedding anniversary, and I didn't think it was a good idea for her to be alone. I had no idea you would react like this. I mean—"

Clyde sat down, pulling her next to him. "Tony has only been dead for a few months. Margie... Margie was never close the others in the group, and she's the kind of woman who needs someone to care for her. They didn't have any children. Tony was her everything, maybe too much so."

"All spouses go through that after death. But it doesn't explain why you—"

"It was her first anniversary without him. It will be her first Christmas without him... New Year's...birthday. She was overwhelmed. She's moving to Florida with her sister soon. She recently sold the home they shared for forty years. You know what that's like."

She did know how Margie must be feeling, but the image of the hug and kiss still bothered her. "Ruth, do you really believe I'd ask you to dinner and let another woman come in and...interrupt our evening? Seventy is slapping me in the face, that's a little old to be a player. Besides, I don't have the game, money or the energy."

Ruth felt a little silly. If it was a triangle, Margie was the one who should have been mad. "When I saw—"

"You saw an old friend consoling an old friend."

The fact that Margie was moving to Florida put it all in perspective.

"Are we all right now or do I need to get a notarized statement from Margie?" He reached out for her, and she stood, took the three steps to him that seemed like a mile.

Just as they embraced, Allison entered. She cleared her throat. "Good evening, forgive the interruption. I'm Allison, Ruth's daughter-in-law and you must be Clyde." She extended her hand, "It's nice to meet you."

"Very nice to meet you too," he said, shaking her hand. "I met your husband the other night. Beautiful family. Well, I better be going."

"Oh, don't let me run you off. Would you like to stay for dinner?"

"Thank you but maybe another time. I have a lodge meeting tonight. It was nice meeting you. Ruth, I'll call you later." Ruth smiled as she walked him to the door. "Are we all right?"

Ruth nodded.

He kissed her goodbye and this time she didn't pull away.

Allison smiled as Ruth entered the kitchen. "The way he looked at you, even when he was talking to me, somebody's been caught."

The next few months, Clyde and Ruth were back on track with phone calls, emails, and everything else. In fact, they helped Margie pack for her move. She and Clyde still hadn't put a name to their relationship and she was okay with that for now.

Clyde invited Ruth to the birthday get together his family threw for him each year. This would be the first time she'd meet his kids and grandchildren. They were a beautiful family. She loved watching the way he interacted with different generations of them. Listening to their memories of their mother helped her understand his devotion to family. She checked her watch, shocked that it was after two in the morning. She reached for her phone to text Davis, but it was dead. She knew he would be worried and stood to leave.

Concerned about her driving alone late at night, Clyde told her to leave her car and he'd drive her home.

Paulette quickly offered to drive with him, and Ruth agreed.

They hadn't been in the car more than ten minutes when they heard Clyde snoring. Paulette laughed. "Dad would always do that when we went on trips. As soon as Mama took the wheel, he was out. You're going to have to navigate to your house. I'm not familiar with that area."

"Okay, it's not hard."

Paulette put on her blinker. "Dad seemed worried about you driving. I thought you might be sick or something."

"Not sick, just not used to driving at night. Turn right at the next intersection."

"He only has on a light jacket. I hope he doesn't catch a cold. He forgets that he's not young anymore." Following Ruth's directions, Paulette pulled into a driveway. "Is this it?"

Ruth nodded and gathered her things." Do you want your dad to get in the front?"

Paulette shook her head.

"Then I won't wake him. Thank you for driving me home. Tell your dad I said goodnight."

Paulette smiled. "No problem. We'll see you in the morning."

"In the morning?" Ruth asked puzzled.

"When you come pickup your car."

Ruth had forgotten about leaving her car that quickly. "Right. Tomorrow."

She flicked the porch lights as soon as she entered, so Paulette would know she was safe. She turned to find Davis and Allison descending on her like troopers.

Davis' nostrils were twice their normal size. "Mother, do you have any idea what time it is?"

Ruth understood his concern but not his anger. "Clyde's family arrived tonight, and they're preparing for his get together."

"That's fine for his family, but you are our family and we were worried about you. We didn't know if you'd gotten sick or been in an accident..."

"I'm sorry. I didn't mean to worry you. The time got away from me and my phone died on top of that. I do apologize."

"He doesn't have a land line? You couldn't borrow someone's phone? That was irresponsible, Ruth." Allison scolded as she and Davis turned and stomped up the stairs.

The next morning, Davis and Allison were seated at the breakfast table. Ruth's cheerful 'good morning' was met with a barely audible greeting until Davis looked out the window. "Mother, your car isn't in the driveway! How did—"

"It was late, Davis. I left my car at Clyde's. I'm going to get this morning. He'll pick me up shortly and—"

"Get your purse. I'll take you." His voice was firm.

Ruth rolled her eyes and grabbed her purse. *You would think I was the child.* She followed Davis to the garage, and they rode to Clyde's in silence.

When they arrived, she turned to Davis. "Thank you. I'll be home a little later."

Davis stared straight ahead. "I'll wait."

Ruth was close to losing her temper. "Davis, I don't need you to wait for me. I am perfectly capable of driving myself home."

"I know you can drive home. You just don't seem to know *when* to drive home."

Ruth exited the car and said calmly, "I will see you at home...later."

Everyone smiled and waved, even those she didn't know as she entered the house. She heard somebody holler 'fifteen' and knew she was near the domino table.

Ruth found Paulette in the kitchen.

"The only thing I have to do is make his cherry cobbler, I already have the Blue Bell," Paulette smiled.

"Cobbler and not a birthday cake?"

"There'll be a cake, but it's for the rest of us. Daddy loves warm cherry cobbler with a scoop of Blue Bell homemade vanilla ice cream on top. Every year, Mama would make him his own cherry cobbler. I've continued the tradition. Thank goodness, I'm a better baker than I am a cook."

Every spot on the five burner stove was covered. Ruth offered to help, but Paulette said there were too many booties in the kitchen already.

She made her way to the backyard. The yard was filled with smoke as the self-proclaimed pit masters opened the tops of several pits to check their meat.

Clyde gave up his spot when he saw her. Seeing she was upset, he led her away from the smoke and people. "Is everything okay?"

Ruth nodded her head as tears welled in her eyes. Embarrassed about crying, she apologized and turned to leave. Clyde reached for her hand, and they sat on the bench on the side of the house.

"Never apologize for being human, Ruth, and you never have to be embarrassed about letting me know how you're feeling."

Paulette came around the corner. "I'm sorry. There's someone asking for Ruth."

"It's Davis. He's upset about my coming in so late last night. He refused to leave when he dropped me off. He's been sitting in his car all this time." She stood. "I guess I better go."

Clyde pulled her back down. "Sit. Let me go talk to Davis, man to man. Hopefully, that will ease his mind about us."

Ruth shook her head. "No, Clyde, I don't want my problems to spoil your celebration."

"Davis needs to know how I feel about you, how special you are to me and whether he likes it or not, we are going to be together. And he might as well know it now." Clyde walked away.

"Ruth, can I speak to you for a minute?" Paulette sat next to her. "I'm concerned about my dad. Did Dad tell you he spent the last two years of my mother's life taking care of her? It really took a toll on him. He's just beginning to get back to his old self." Paulette rubbed her hands up and down her thighs as she talked. "You're the first woman he has shown any real interest in. Letting you meet the family, spending so much time with you... He's dated other women, but we knew he wasn't serious about them."

"And now you feel he may be getting... serious?"

"My concern, and I mean no disrespect, is that you seem to come with... baggage. At this time in my father's life, he doesn't need any drama. He needs to be happy." Paulette hesitated. "I'm sure you're a nice lady, but I'm very protective of my father, and I won't let anyone hurt him."

"Paulette, I assure you, I would never do anything to hurt your dad, but I appreciate your honesty. I'm sure this wasn't easy for you."

Paulette looked at Ruth and grimaced. She stood and walked away without looking back.

Ruth would have to process this conversation later, right now, she needed to check on Davis and Clyde. She waded through the crowd to the front door. The two men were talking inside Davis's car.

Clyde opened the door as she approached. "Davis and I have had an enlightening talk. I think we understand each other a little better now."

Ruth looked at Davis, who was adjusting his seat belt. "Are you okay?"

"I'm fine. Are your leaving now or are you going to stay for a while?"

"I'd like to stay for a bit."

"Then I'll see you at home."

Clyde patted Ruth's back as Davis pulled off. "I think more than anything, he is worried about losing you."

"That was all you talked about?"

Clyde steered Ruth to his office when they entered the house. They sat in dark brown leather chairs facing each other. "I shared with Davis about my marriage and Deborah's illness. I told him that you are the first woman that I have really been interested in since her death. I care about you, Ruth, and I don't mean just as a friend. I really care about you, the way a man cares about a woman. I didn't think that would happen again after Deborah, but it has. Am I the only one feeling this way?" When Ruth failed to respond, Clyde stood and pulled her into his arms. "If I'm wrong, I need you to tell me now." He kissed her quickly, and then slowly and passionately.

Ruth hadn't been kissed like that since before Martin got sick. Clyde stepped back and caressed her arms.

Ruth knew she wasn't sixteen, but she surely felt like it. Her breath was shallow, and she was tingling all over.

"You're not wrong." She kissed him as passionately as he had kissed her, and they held onto each other without speaking.

There was a knock at the door. "Dad?" Paulette called out as she entered. She stopped short. "Oh, excuse me. I'm sorry, but the food is ready and the kids are whining, some adults too. Can you come bless the food so we can eat?"

Clyde and Ruth let out a slow breath and released each other just as slowly. "Okay, we're coming." He took Ruth's hand and led her out.

There was a collective 'amen' after the prayer as the people grabbed for plates before Paulette stopped them.

"Shouldn't the birthday boy be the first one to eat?" She pointed at her dad.

Clyde shook his head. "Let them go ahead, I'm in no hurry."

Paulette ignored him as she prepared his plate. "Since it's your special day, I'm going to relax the dietary restrictions...a little." He smiled as she added baked chicken and dressing, collard greens, macaroni and cheese, and candied yams to his plate.

"Here you go, but take it easy, okay? Ruth, would you like me to fix your plate?"

"Yes," Clyde said. "She's a special guest... this year." A few of the kids asked if that meant she couldn't come back next year.

Clyde chuckled. "Don't worry about what it means, just get your plate. The picnic tables are for the small kids and the teens can eat in the tent. And, don't be throwing anything in the fire pit!"

Everyone ate, laughed, joked, and shared more tender memories. It was a beautiful birthday celebration. Several times, during dinner, Ruth noticed Clyde looking at her.

After dinner, Clyde signaled Ruth to follow him. They went to one of the bedrooms that had been converted to a lounge. "This is my getaway when the family gets to be too much for me. Sit." He adjusted one of the pillows behind her. "You can put your feet up if you want to. I love it when they come home, but I also love to see them leave.

It is nonstop when they are here, and when you are used to being alone most of the time, all that activity and noise gets old."

Ruth nodded. "I'm sure, but I love seeing the way you are with your family."

He laughed, "When the kids were growing up, we didn't have much, but we had love. All the neighborhood kids hung out here."

"They felt the love. That was more important than things...and space."

Clyde rubbed his red eyes and then his head. Ruth could tell he was tired. "It's getting late. I think I better go." She reached for her shoes, but he put his arm out.

"Don't go yet." He turned on the stereo.

Ruth didn't know much about jazz but she knew what she liked.

"You want to dance?"

Ruth smiled. "Maybe another time. Tomorrow is going to be a long day. What time does the party start?"

He laughed. "Baby, the party has already started. This will go nonstop until Sunday night."

He lowered the volume on the music. When she looked at him again, his head was back, and he was out. She kissed him on his forehead, gathered her shoes and purse and eased out of the room.

A few minutes before eleven, she pulled in her driveway. The house was so quiet, she figured everybody was asleep or pretending to be. She went to bed, she needed to rest for the party tomorrow.

When she arrived the next afternoon, his family, friends, neighbors, classmates, former co-workers were all there. There were so many people, Ruth couldn't see Clyde. Finally, he came out of the garage looking sharp in his chino dress pants and short sleeved sweater. He smiled when he spotted her. "I was wondering where you were."

He pulled her into the lounge. "I don't know if it's because I'm getting old or they are getting louder, but this is too much noise for me. We can go somewhere else if you want to."

"You need to rest for a little while. Lean back and relax while you have a minute. They'd be hurt if you left after they've gone through all this trouble."

"Look out that door. I'll give you fifty dollars if you can find two square feet of unoccupied space. They wouldn't miss me; they wouldn't even know if I was gone."

He sat next to her and entwined their fingers. "I want you to understand something, when we raised our kids, we gave them everything we had to equip them for life. For the most part, they have not disappointed me. I don't think there is anything wrong with putting myself at the top of my list at this point."

"I'm not saying it's wrong, but they may not be prepared for you to make serious life changes."

"Dad," Paulette knocked on the door, before entering the room. "It's after two, time to eat. I just took the cherry cobbler out of the oven, and the ice cream is on the counter."

Clyde smiled. "She doesn't play fair. She knows that cherry cobbler would make me leave an operating table."

In true celebration of his birthday, Paulette placed birthday candles in the cherry cobbler. Clyde took a huge serving and told her to hide the rest, and everyone laughed.

Paul had the DJ make an Al Green playlist, Clyde's favorite singer. Clyde danced with his youngest great granddaughter and a few of the older neighbors. He finally danced with her as *Love and Happiness played.*

Ruth was impressed, he still had some moves. She stayed a little longer, and then went home despite Clyde's request that she stay.

Even after Davis and Clyde's conversation, there was some tension in her house about their relationship. With the holiday season coming, Ruth felt torn between the two families. She started secretly house hunting, believing it was time for her to move out and get a place of her own.

After several weeks of looking, she found a condo she thought might work for her. She decided to tell Clyde about her hunt and asked him to meet her at the condo to see the space.

"Why are you looking at a place with stairs?" He asked.

When Ruth didn't respond, he tried again. "Ruth, are you upset that I asked about the stairs? We both have trouble with our knees, and I just thought...never mind." He put his hands in his pockets and followed silently as she continued the tour.

Clyde didn't say anything until the tour was over. "The backyard is really small. A pit won't fit back there. HOA fees will add more than two thousand dollars a year—"

"This is why I didn't tell you I was looking for my own place. I knew you'd be critical."

"All I'm saying is there are things you need to consider. Buying a house is a big deal. You should get what you want. That master bedroom closet can't hold my clothes let alone yours."

"That won't be a problem since you won't be bringing your clothes over here. How dare you presume that I am buying a house so you can move in."

"That wasn't what I was saying and you know it. If that was an issue, I would have asked you to move into my house."

"Clyde, do you believe for one second that I'd move into your house and live with the scorn of your daughter and the ghost of your wife?" Ruth knew she had crossed the line, but before she could apologize, Clyde got in his car and pulled off.

When she got home, she finished the dinner, visited with Martin for a few minutes and went to bed. She tossed and turned until three in the morning. She needed to be honest with herself about why she was acting this way. The truth was she was scared. Scared. Scared to move out on her own. Scared about her relationship with Clyde, just scared.

Sleep never came, when Ruth looked at the clock again, it was six o'clock. Too early to call Clyde and apologize. By ten, she'd left several messages and still hadn't heard from him. An hour later, her phone rang. "I wondered when you would finally be ready to talk to me."

"Is this Ruth Willis?"

Ruth didn't recognize the voice. "Yes, this is Ruth Willis." Caller ID said it was Clyde's phone, why was a woman calling from his phone asking for her? Ruth could hear a lot of noise in the background.

"This is Beverly Sanders. I work in Social Services at Madison General. Do you know a Mr. Clyde Anderson?"

She closed her eyes and held her breath, "Yes, I know Mr. Anderson. Is there a problem? Where is Clyde?" Ruth heard papers rattling.

"Just a moment, please," the lady said.

The lady said something about next of kin and Ruth's heart skipped a beat. "Can you tell me what this is concerning?"

The woman returned to the line. "I'm sorry, ma'am, are you related to Mr. Anderson?"

"He... he is a dear friend. Can I speak to him?"

"I'm sorry, but Mr. Anderson has suffered a medical episode and has been admitted to the hospital."

Ruth heard her heart beating outside of her body. "I am on my way."

"Ms. Willis, do you have the number of a family member? You were in his phone as his emergency contact, but our regulations say that we can only talk to a family member unless we have a signed consent form to do otherwise."

"His children's numbers are in his phone. Look for Paulette James or Josh or Benjamin Anderson. I'm on my way."

Ruth hung up before the woman could respond. She didn't care about any rules or regulations, nothing was going to keep her from seeing Clyde. She dressed as fast as she could and told Allison where she going as she rushed out the door.

Praying as she pulled into the parking garage, it dawned on her that she hadn't asked for a room number. The attendant at the visitor's desk told her he was in ICU, room 327. Stepping off the elevator on the third floor, she saw Paulette, Josh and Benjamin.

When she reached them, Benjamin was on his cell phone updating his brothers and Paulette was fighting back tears. Ruth hugged her and led her to a chair. "They don't know anything yet. They think it might be a heart attack, but the doctors are running more tests." Paulette said.

Ruth didn't want to appear intrusive. She remembered the hurt look on his face the last time they spoke. *Lord, please, don't let it end like this. Please.* An hour passed before one of the doctors updated them. Clyde was stable, he'd been given a sedative and was resting. A cardiologist was reviewing the test results they'd run earlier. He suggested they leave their contact information with the nurse, go home and get some rest. The staff would notify them of any changes in Clyde's condition.

They thanked him, knowing that no one was leaving. As the night went on, Paulette and Josh dozed, and Benjamin went to get them something to eat.

Benjamin returned with a bucket of chicken. No one was hungry. One of the aides was nice enough to bring them blankets and pillows, and each of them dozed off and on until daylight.

Not able to wait any longer, Ruth snuck in his room during shift change. She froze. He was connected to so many machines, tubes, and oxygen. Images of Martin just before he died flashed through her mind. A signal went off and several nurses ran into the room. One nurse told Ruth that she had to leave as the other nurses checked the equipment. Ruth went back to the waiting room.

Ruth moved to the chair by the window. The congested highway wasn't much of a view, but she was thinking more than looking anyway. Seeing Clyde like that brought back the fear and anxiety she had experienced during Martin's illness. She felt as helpless now as she did then.

At eight o'clock, a nurse told the family the doctor wanted to see them. Paulette, Benjamin and Josh gathered their things, folded the blankets and stood by the door. Ruth was still sitting when the nurse returned.

The three of them started through the doors to ICU when Paulette looked back.

"She said he wanted to talk to the family," Ruth said.

Paulette went back and picked up Ruth's purse and pulled her up. "You are family."

They walked slowly down the hallway. Their dread turned to relief when they entered his room and Clyde was not only awake but alert. The doctor explained that it wasn't a heart attack at all. Clyde had suffered an anxiety attack exacerbated by his high blood pressure.

"You're not getting rid of me that easily." Clyde's voice was raspy. He remained in the hospital three days, and they ran additional tests to make sure they hadn't overlooked anything. Ruth and Paulette tag-teamed staying at the hospital, and the boys came and went. The other children who lived out of state called him every day. Even Davis and Allison came to see him.

The third day of Clyde's hospital stay, Ruth was home drinking tea. Like a dam breaking without warning, suddenly, she was crying and couldn't stop. All she could envision was day after day after day of watching her Martin slip away. And though Clyde's prognosis was good, she couldn't get over her fear of what might happen. She loved Clyde, but she just couldn't go through the emotional upheaval again.

Allison saw her crying and told her it was a release. Clyde was doing fine and things would be back to normal again. "No, things will never be normal again. This is how it started with Martin, and he just went downhill until there was nothing left." Ruth shook her head. "I can't deal with this again."

Allison reached for Ruth's hand, which was uncharacteristic. "You and I have our differences, there is no getting around that. But, you are one of the strongest women I know. I watched you take care of a dying man with such tenderness and hope as if he was going to live a hundred years. You handled all of your financial and legal affairs as though you'd done it your entire life — without a complaint. I understand you're scared, Ruth, but if I don't know anything else about your relationship with Clyde Anderson, I know that he loves you and that you love him. So, go ahead and let those tears out. Have your moment of doubt, take a deep breath, wash your face...and go take care of your man."

Ruth rested for an hour, changed clothes and went back to the hospital. Paulette left to get her kids as soon as Ruth arrived. Clyde woke up when his lunch tray arrived.

"I can tell you're feeling better. Your color is coming back." They both laughed. Ruth wanted to apologize about the argument but was afraid of upsetting him.

"Something is bothering you. What is it? The doctor said I'll be fine in a few weeks. In time for Thanksgiving. Then, I can really show you what I can do."

Ruth offered him a weak smile.

"What is it, sweetheart? This isn't about my being in here, is it?"

Ruth stared out the window. "I sat by Martin's bedside day in and day out, watching life slip away from him. I didn't resent it; I was his wife. My place was by his side. But just as life was slipping out of him, it was slipping out of me too. It was a pain I couldn't explain to anyone."

"I felt the same way watching Deborah. I was still holding her hand an hour later after she transitioned."

"When the hospital called me that first night, I snuck in here to see you and I froze. I knew it was you, but it was like watching Martin all over again and... Clyde, I don't know if I can... if I can go... I know this isn't the time to discuss this, but..."

He pushed the control to raise his head. Ruth came to him, but he put up his hand to stop her. "I'm good." He adjusted himself and turned to face her.

"I understand. That's why it's taken me so long to let myself care about another woman. When Deborah died, she weighed eighty-two pounds. When she was healthy, the smallest size she wore was a fourteen. Every day, I told her how beautiful she was...and I wasn't lying. She was still beautiful to me." He took a drink of water. "I never gave up. And you didn't give up with Martin. And you shouldn't give up now."

She shook her head. "After our argument about the condo and the way you drove off... I thought... I was so wrong."

"Look, we are going to disagree. But we can't let the way we feel about a situation change the way we feel about each other." He looked away. "Maybe we... I was moving too fast. It's just that for the first time in a long time, I feel so alive when you're around. But I don't think we need to make any big decisions just yet. So, we'll save the change of address cards for now." He reached for her hand. "Okay?"

"Okay."

"Now, do you think you could find me some cherry cobbler and Blue Bell ice cream around here?"

The weeks passed, and Clyde looked better than ever as the holiday festivities began. Hoping Davis and Allison wouldn't feel out of place at Clyde's Christmas party, Ruth introduced them to people she thought they'd like. Clyde pulled her to the side and told her they were perfectly capable of choosing their own friends. He was right. She stopped and soon realized they got along fine with everyone.

Christmas at the Anderson's house was something to experience. His home, including the front and back yard, was beautifully decorated for the season. Three full sized Christmas trees filled the inside of the house. One was set up in the garage for the under twenty-one crowd. Multi-colored flashing lights, homemade ornaments, streams of garland and a large train ran around the base of it. Gifts were placed carefully under and around the tree with fingers crossed that no one derailed the train. The tree in the living room, was decorated with multi-colored lights like the other tree, but the decorations were traditional and older for their special guests. Their family's Christmas tradition included celebrating with their neighbors and the senior members of the church who resided in nursing homes or assisted living facilities. They coordinated with the church and nursing home staffs to make sure that all the residents had at least two gifts and a Christmas stocking filled with a Christmas card, a small ornament, and fruit and candy for those who were allowed. For those who couldn't have the fruit and candy, a special ornament or small book was added to their stocking. There were also gift certificates for spas, restaurants, and local businesses for the caregivers.

Clyde wanted to show Ruth his special Christmas tree in his office, but Ruth protested.

"Sooner or later, you are going to have to accept that you are not 'just another guest'. You are not like anyone else, Ruth Willis. Besides, your presents are under this tree."

"You shouldn't have done that. I mean, this is special family time. ... I don't want your kids thinking I am trying to replace—"

"Ruth, that health scare only reaffirmed my decision to do what makes me happy. And, a large part of what makes me happy is you." He wrapped his arms around her and placed his forehead against hers.

Every time Ruth registered a complaint, he kissed her. She tried to pull back, but he wouldn't relax his grip. By the time she lodged her third objection, she found herself kissing him back.

There was a knock at the door. Clyde took a deep breath. "I'm getting a 'DO NOT DISTURB' sign to put on that door. Yes?"

The door opened.

Clyde stared up at Benjamin, who easily stood a half foot taller than Clyde. "I said 'yes', I didn't say come in."

Benjamin chuckled. "Seems I was chosen to be the sacrificial lamb. Anyway, the family says you and Miss Ruth are MIA and it's time for the kids open their presents and sing Christmas carols."

"Tell them we're coming."

Benjamin didn't move.

"I said we'll be there in a minute."

Benjamin hesitated, and Clyde gave him a 'Dad' face. "You want to test me on Christmas, boy?"

"No, sir, but your daughter told me, under threat of severe pain, not to come back without you."

Even Ruth had to laugh. Clyde gently pushed Ruth out the door. When they entered the living room everyone started cheering.

Ruth and Clyde looked at one another and shrugged.

"Okay, so what's the deal here? Those presents are already opened." Clyde asked, scanning the room.

All of the kids turned to the side, and Paulette stepped forward with a box. "We know that it's been a difficult time for you, for both of you. So, we got together and got you a special gift. A cruise to... St. Croix!"

Clyde and Ruth fell against each other laughing as they opened the box to find suntan oil and floral shirts. They thanked everyone and watched the kids play with their gifts. They slipped back to the other room when the music started again. Clyde was still chuckling.

Reaching under the cushion of the loveseat, he handed Ruth an envelope. Ruth was puzzled as she opened the envelope because they had exchanged gifts earlier. She shook her head and smiled, now Clyde's laughter made sense.

"What are we going to do with two pairs of tickets to St. Croix? Take another couple with us?"

Clyde held her tight. "Well, I was thinking one cruise could be to celebrate our engagement and we can use the other for our honeymoon."

"What?" Ruth pushed against his chest. "We aren't engaged!"

Clyde kissed her and reached into his pants pocket, "Christmas isn't over yet."

About the Author

Jeanette W. Hill is the founder and executive director of JWHill Productions, a theatrical production company and Sight Ain't Seeing Productions, a 501(C) 3 creative arts nonprofit organization that serves under-represented and under-served communities.

The award-winning playwright (*The Best Lesson, Dealing with Daddy's Devils and The Silent City*) seamlessly combines the best of traditional with urban theater. From a business perspective, Hill is a firm believer that art does not have to bow down to profit or lack of quality to be entertaining.

Jeanette Hill was featured in the documentary, *Black and Write*, and selected to participate in the D.C. Black Theatre Festival. She is the 2013 recipient of the Kingdomwood Christian Film Festival's, "People's Choice Award for a Stage Play," and the winner of the renowned Atlanta Black Theatre Festival's, "Best Staged Reading" award. And she is a winner of the 2014 Black Pearls Magazine Literary Excellence Awards.

Hill's community activism is demonstrated in the projects she's taken on such as anti-bullying campaigns as well as faith-based initiatives to promote the arts. She is a sought-after workshop facilitator, speaker and conference panelist.

The Akron, Ohio, native currently works and resides with her family in Austin, Texas. Visit her online at jwhillproductions.com.

Reunited
Annie Johnson

Chapter One

Meeting Troy
Chicago, Illinois

"What a difference a day makes," Miranda Jones mumbled. She sat on her patio, sipping on a cup of tea, enjoying her croissant. She was tired of showing up for her own pity party and had decided to smile today. Besides, the sun was shining, and the birds were tweeting, and she was in her favorite place. She tilted her head back and closed her eyes, enjoying the nice breeze.

"Ahhhh," Miranda sighed. No visions of teeth, cavities or impacted gums filled her mind, and thankfully, no visions of Troy. Miranda thought about her brief marriage to Troy.

"Why am I a dentist? I should be a bestselling author. I could easily write a book on *What Not to Do When You Meet A Guy* or *How to Not Get Swept Off Your Feet*." She moved her feet off the ottoman and thought of her best friend, Natalia. "See, Nat? This is what happens when you move to Paris to pursue your dream and leave me here. I end up talking to the birds."

Miranda and Natalia shared a love for jazz. Natalia had moved to Paris, France, to open a jazz dinner club. Miranda was a jazz vocalist, but life in the foster care system had made her somewhat of a pragmatist, so she went to dental school and opened her own practice. Though, she still hoped to one day pursue a career as a jazz vocalist.

Natalia was the kind of friend that would do anything for you, and right up until the day before she moved to Paris, she served as Miranda's dental assistant helping her in her practice.

It was in her dental office that Miranda met Troy. That day she'd almost given herself whiplash trying to get a second look at the handsome man. "Great Scott!" Miranda had always had a habit of talking to herself. "This has got to be the finest man on earth besides Denzel."

She returned to the room where she was extracting a tooth from a patient. Once Miranda finished the extraction, she went into the next room and reviewed the chart Natalia had left with the gentleman's x-ray and information form. "Hmmm, Troy." He wanted to have his teeth cleaned. Miranda looked at the x-ray again, "Beautiful teeth."

There was a knock at the door and Natalia escorted him in. Miranda's heart skipped a beat. The man was gloriously handsome — tall, dark and handsome. He had a bald head, and though he was thin, he was muscular. Miranda could tell he worked out on a regular basis. And, he had the most beautiful brown eyes she'd seen on a man, captivating really. Miranda's palms were sweaty, and she was not normally a nervous person. She wiped her hands against her white coat.

She extended her hand. "Hi, I'm Dr. Jones."

"Hi, I'm Troy." He offered her a firm handshake.

Miranda appreciated that. She was looking for a man who would treat her as an equal. She shook her head. *Um, this was her patient.*

She smiled. "What brings you in, Troy?"

"Routine cleaning."

Miranda nodded and looked at Natalia who had set everything up for her. She smiled at

her friend and then finished her consultation with Troy. As she cleaned his teeth, Miranda noticed him checking her out. She concentrated on her work and tried to appear unbothered, but he was having an effect on her. A good effect.

"Whoo," she said when he left, "I'm not sure how I survived that cleaning. I thought I

would faint with all that gorgeousness staring at me."

Natalia nodded. "He was quite attractive."

"Right? And he lives so close to us. Why have we never seen him before in the sea of

Chicagoans that come and go? According to his chart, his building is only a few doors down from mine."

Natalia laughed. "You peeped the man's address?"

Miranda shrugged her shoulders. "I am not ashamed, my friend. Not ashamed at all. And

who knows? Maybe I'll run into him at the neighborhood gym or something since he lives so close. It's obvious the brother spends a considerable amount of time in the gym."

Natalia shook her head. "I'm not sure if I should be moving to Paris or not. I

think someone needs to watch out for you."

Miranda hugged her friend. "Are you kidding me? You're going to have the most popular

jazz dinner club in all of Paris. I can't wait to visit you in the City of Lights."

When Miranda arrived at work the next morning, there was a big bouquet of beautiful

roses sitting on her desk with a card attached. "Who on earth sent our office flowers?"

To her surprise, the flowers weren't for the office, they were for her from Troy, the handsome patient from yesterday. The card read, *Thank You, Dr. Jones, for the fine work you did on my teeth.*

She squealed with a grin on her face so big she could examine her own teeth. "Oooo, how

thoughtful, this is so sweet." Miranda continued reading the note.

I was hoping you would consider joining me for a drink this evening at the jazz club in the Marina Towers. I'm fully aware that you don't know me, so feel free to bring a friend along. Hope to hear from you, Troy.

Miranda was familiar with the jazz club, she used to go there frequently. In fact, she had performed at the jazz dinner club several times in the past. The venue was divine.

Natalia opened Miranda's office door. "Girl, what are you squealing about? I could hear you down the hall."

Miranda pointed to the roses and then waved the card at her best friend.

Natalia took the card and read it. When she finished, she looked up at Miranda wide eyed. "Oooo, you got an admirer."

Miranda nodded. "Mmm, maybe. Seems innocent enough, you wanna be my chaperone for the evening?"

Natalia smiled. "For you, my friend, anything. Besides, jazz is my entire world. I can't think of a better way to spend the evening."

Miranda called Troy but got his voicemail. "Hey, Troy, this is Dr. Jones, er uh...Miranda. Thank you for the flowers, and I'd love to meet tonight for a drink. I'll be bringing my dental assistant along. You met her yesterday as well. Anyway, we'll see you at the jazz club around seven."

Looking forward to a fun evening, Miranda took extra care in making sure her caramel complexion was flawless. She wore a jumpsuit that accentuated her tall slender body in all the right places without being overly seductive, and then called for Uber. She took the rideshare car to Marina Towers where Natalia was waiting for her out front when she arrived.

The ladies gave their name at the door as Troy had instructed when he called back and were escorted to seats at the front of the club near the stage. To their surprise, Troy came out on the stage with the rest of the band and began to sing. Their eyes met, and he nodded a hello. Miranda smiled and did the same. She was mesmerized by his performance. He was a gifted jazz vocalist. Miranda was mesmerized by his dazzling eyes.

What a coincidence, we're both jazz vocalist. Go figure.

After his set, Troy joined them for dinner and drinks. The three got along well, and the conversation flowed easily since they all loved jazz. Before the night ended, Troy had asked Miranda if she would be willing to share her mobile number with him. Just as she was about to exit the Uber, her phone rang.

Miranda smiled. "Hey, Troy, you home already?"

"I am, and I wanted to make sure you made it home safely."

"I'm just about to walk into my condo now," Miranda unlocked the door and went inside. She disarmed the alarm code and kicked off her shoes. She and Troy talked so long, they almost fell asleep on the phone.

"I should let you go," Troy said. "I'm sure you have a lot to do tomorrow."

"Just work and then the gym."

"Oh yea, what gym do you go to?"

"XSport Fitness on State. I like that they're twenty-four hours."

Troy laughed. "Why have we not met before yesterday? That's my gym too. I'm usually there in the morning though. Wanna meet tomorrow afternoon and workout together? I'd love to have you as my partner... uh, my workout partner."

"Yea, I'd like that."

Miranda and Troy became inseparable. She tried to keep her wits about her. She had just met him and knew next to nothing about him, but it didn't stop her from falling in love fast and hard. Troy swept her off her feet. They talked on the telephone until the wee hours of the morning. They went on dates, and the fact that they both were jazz enthusiasts and vocalists only drew them closer together.

After an eight-month courtship, despite Natalia's attempts to convince Miranda to slow down and plan a nice wedding, they married downtown at City Hall with Natalia as their witness. Who needed a fancy elaborate wedding when you were in love? All Miranda wanted was to honeymoon in Hawaii with Troy.

How could she possibly know a whirlwind romance would lead to catastrophic heartbreak?

She never expected to walk into their condo one day and find Troy and all his belongings gone.

Just like her days in the Cook County Foster Care system, quick as a snap of a finger, things changed. Miranda didn't have any family, at least none that she knew about. She carried an old picture of her birth mother in her wallet. She knew her mom lived in California and planned to look for her someday. Troy had told her he would help her with the search. She was told that her birth mother hung around the wrong people doing the wrong things and didn't think she would be able to raise Miranda properly, so she gave her up. Miranda entered the foster care system and was pushed around from home to home until she aged out.

Miranda had thrown herself across the bed, crying into a pillow that smelled of his cologne. "Will the story of my life always be one of abandonment?"

We were in love. How could he leave? Why did he leave?

Devastated, Miranda cried until her eyes were red and swollen. Some part of her wanted to blame herself, like she always did whenever she would come home from school and find her caseworker waiting at one of her foster homes.

What had she done wrong this time? She always tried to be a good girl.

Miranda sat up and wiped her face with the back of her hand. "No, this is not on me. I didn't do anything wrong." She reached for the tissue box on her nightstand and spotted an envelope with her name on it. She picked it up and broke the seal, unfolding the stationery inside.

Dear Miranda, I love you more than words can say. No, I do not have another woman. No, me leaving has nothing to do with anything you have done. Currently, I feel like less of a man. I love my career, but I am unable to keep you in the manner that you are accustomed to and I feel bad about that. It is not fair that I travel pursuing my career while you continue to work doing something you're not passionate about knowing your love for music is just as strong as mine. The thought of you paying most of our bills drives me insane, and I cannot stand it. As a true man, this just does not seem right to me. I am transitioning from vocalist to songwriter and need to stay in California for a while.

Trust me, once I get established, I will contact you. I love you. If there was any other way for me to make this work... But I need to do what I know to do. Please trust me, Miranda. Love, Troy.

Miranda tossed the note onto the bed and called Natalia.

"Hey, girl, what's up?" Natalia greeted her.

Miranda sniffled. "Nat, Troy left me. He—"

"Wait. What? Stop right there. Hang up, I'll be there in twenty minutes."

When Natalia knocked on the door, Miranda fell in her arms and started crying all over

again. Natalia let Miranda lean against her and walked her over to the couch. She held Miranda and rubbed her back until she calmed down.

"Thank you," Miranda said when Natalia handed her some tissue. "Nat, I'm so glad you

happened to be in town. What would I have done if you were in Paris right now?"

Natalia had been back and forth between Chicago and Paris getting her business set up. After years of saving and planning, she was finally opening a jazz dinner club in France. "You feel like talking about it?"

"I don't know, Nat. I feel... abandoned. We're married. If he felt this way, why didn't he talk to me about it? He should be able to talk to me about anything. That's what couples do. What am I supposed to do, Nat? You're gone. Troy's gone..."

Miranda felt overwhelmed and confused. She shook her head, her mind shocked by her circumstances. "I should have taken your advice, Nat, and gotten to know Troy better before marrying him. I was just so head over heels in love with him... still am."

She bawled up pillow and crushed it against her stomach. She had been abandoned way too many times in her life, and in the wake of Troy's departure, the old feelings from being passed from foster home to foster home resurfaced. "If we were so in love, we should have been able to work things out."

A few months after he disappeared, Miranda realized Troy was apparently working because hefty checks started arriving in her mail from him. Months and months went by, and other than these checks, Miranda still had not heard from Troy. So, she hired a private detective friend to locate Troy so she could serve him with divorce papers. Within days, her friend Justin provided her with Troy's address and contact information in Los Angeles, along with his work address at a prestigious record company. Justin assured her that Troy was not dating anyone.

Please with her detective friend's work Miranda decided she would hire him in the future to look for her mother. Now she had way too much to deal with and it was time to heal from the heartbreak Troy left her.

Chapter Two

Bonjour!
Chicago, Illinois to Paris, France

Miranda called Natalia. "Hey, friend, the deed is done. I'm officially a divorcee."

"Girl, stop. You're young. There's a whole lot more living God has for you to do. In fact, why don't you move to Paris and get started? I need a jazz vocalist for the club and I can't think of anyone better to headline for me. What do you say?"

Miranda was stunned. She knew someday she would close her practice and really pursue her dream of becoming a jazz vocalist. And now, Natalia had made her an offer she couldn't refuse. She would get to sing and be with her best friend again. "Girl, I don't know what to say."

"Say you'll consider it," Natalia encouraged. "I'm serious, Miranda. Give it some thought. I'll get my real estate agent to help you find the perfect place here. We can dine on baguettes and enjoy French coffee together by day, and then at night, the stage will be yours."

"Natalia, I love you. I truly do. And you know I'd give almost anything to be in the same city with you again. Let me think on it. You know me, ever pragmatist."

Natalia chuckled. "I know. It's part of why I love you, bestie. And I'll let you go. I'm sure you're already reaching for your notebook to make a list."

The friends chuckled and said their goodbyes.

Miranda made her a cappuccino and grabbed her favorite notebook. She moved to her peaceful patio, her favorite spot to think and ponder. She wrote down the pros and cons. For the life of her, she could not think of any reason not to take Natalia up on her offer. She had a dream job opportunity set up for her in the city of lights. There was nothing in Chicago to keep her from going after her dream. She was no longer married, she didn't have any children, and would have no problem selling the space she bought for her dental practice and starting a new career. A career she had always dreamed of. A career she had vowed to seriously pursue someday.

It was time to get out of her comfort zone and head to Paris, France, and live her dream. She'd spent enough time having a pity party.

She picked up the telephone and called Natalia. "Yes," she shouted when her friend answered. "I'm coming to Paris."

"Are you serious?" Natalia yelped. "You're really going to take me up on my offer? Oh, Miranda, I am so happy for you and so excited for me. You're going to be a great asset to my organization. I can't think of anyone more perfect than you for this position."

Miranda laughed. "I'm so excited we'll be together again. And you know me, I have my notebook out. So tell me about the practical steps for readying myself for the move."

Natalia and Miranda spent the rest of the call discussing visas and paperwork.

Miranda immediately had her birth certificate translated. Natalia gave her the name of the specialist that took care of all her paperwork before she moved to Paris, and Miranda was grateful for the referral. She sold her dental practice and gave referrals to all her patients. She found employment for all her office workers to make sure they were well taken care of. Miranda shopped for a home online with the assistance of Natalia and her real estate agent. She only had one special request.

She did not want a small house with small rooms like some Parisian homes. She wanted

spacious large rooms. She had visited Natalia in Paris on numerous occasions and knew exactly what she wanted. The real estate agent assured her in her price range there would be an abundance of room in her house. Miranda had Natalia visit the various properties for her. Natalia recorded her walk through of the properties and sent the videos to Miranda. Once she narrowed her choices, she flew to Paris to look at her top three properties and make a final decision. There was no turning back.

Miranda picked a house near the city center. Close to the action. Loaded with French

charm. Rustic décor. Open floor concept. Three bedrooms. Two baths. A patio with nice outdoor

space. A garden. Near café's and shops. Miranda sold her condo and off to Paris she went.

On her last night in the Windy City, Miranda took a stroll down the magnificent mile after leaving a small going away gathering one of her friend's hosted for her. Having been raised in Chicago, she would miss the hustle and bustle of her hometown. She would miss her friends, but she would not miss the sub-zero freezing winter weather. She smiled and headed home for her last night in Chicago.

The next morning, she looked around her empty condominium one more time, and then locked the door before heading to the airport for her flight to Paris, France.

The day Miranda moved into her Paris house, she and Natalia danced around the house in

excitement. They spent so much time at the Le Marais and the Place Vendome shopping until they had the house decorated to perfection.

One afternoon when Natalia was visiting, Miranda had prepared a surprise for her friend. "Nat, I can't thank you enough. I really appreciate all you've done to help me transition from the States to Paris. I have something for you."

She handed her friend a rectangular velvet blue box.

Natalia loosened the white bow and opened the box, and then she looked at her friend, tears springing into her eyes. "Oh, Miranda, this is so extravagant." Inside the box was a diamond necklace with the letter N.

Miranda shook her head. "You are the best friend a girl could have. You had everything planned out, so I could see and experience all that Paris had to offer. I could never repay you. Please accept my gift."

Natalia took Miranda to see Notre Dame Cathedral and the Louvre art museum. Miranda found it beautiful. They went on several boat tours. Her favorite was the Seine River Cruise. This was a great way to see the city. They attended several shows during Paris fashion week. They went to every café in Paris. Miranda lived within walking distance of tons of cafés, outdoor markets and restaurants and quickly became hooked on the food and pastries. Miranda was like a kid in a candy factory.

The bread and pastries could not be beat. She soon found that everything she'd heard about the food in France is true.

Miranda finished savory the pastry on her plate. As she wiped her mouth with a napkin, she commented, "Natalia, I have to put an end to all of this eating."

Natalia laughed, "I understand. When I first moved to Paris, I ate seafood. Meaning whenever I saw food, girl, I ate it."

They both fell out laughing at Miranda's attempt at humor.

She held up a finger. "Then I learned the secret, of how Parisians stay thin. I quickly adopted the French practice of making lunch the biggest meal of the day. This makes a big difference."

Miranda nodded, making note of this tip on how she could eat herself into oblivion.

After settling in Paris, Miranda soon became the featured artist at Natalia's jazz dinner club. She was living her dream and enjoyed performing. The small intimate venue was very successful and always packed. Many of the gentlemen that came to see the show expressed interest in her. She occasionally went out to dinner or to a show, but after Troy, dating was not a top priority for her.

Chapter Three

Troy
Los Angeles, California

Troy was in California, performing and writing, hobnobbing with the big-time
music moguls on the Hollywood scene. He was connected to all the right people in all the right places. No one was surprised that he turned out to be successful. He was super talented and it was obvious to everyone he had a special talent. However, in his personal life, he was missing something. Troy was missing his wife, his ex-wife, and wanted to reconnect with her.

Although Troy loved Los Angeles, he knew it was time for him to seek out Miranda. He had to make things right between them. He decided it would be wise to keep his apartment in California because there would be times when spending time in L.A. would be necessary for business. Not often, but periodically.

He went back to Chicago and was surprised Miranda had given up her dental practice. He was even more taken aback when he learned Miranda had moved to Paris. After he thought about it, he wasn't that surprised. Miranda had always expressed an interest in the Parisian jazz scene and often went on extended visits there with her friend Natalia. Troy remembered her speaking about how she loved the vintage grand architecture.

He was surprised when he received the divorce papers. He had no idea Miranda would divorce him. He loved her and had her best interest in mind when he left. He had a feeling he was going to have a tough time convincing her of that, but he was glad she had pursued the career of her dreams. He wanted her to be happy and fulfilled.

Troy picked up the telephone and called his assistant. He had his assistant arrange travel and find a place in Paris to live. He was going to find his ex-wife and get her back in his life. He knew it would not be easy, but he was still in love with Miranda and always would be. He was willing to do whatever he needed to do. He felt like a fool, but he was determined to fight with every fiber of his being to re-earn her trust, her love, and to reunite with his one and only true love, Miranda.

He had all the money he ever wanted, but one thing money couldn't buy was love. When he left Miranda to come to California, he had good intentions, but he realized he should have taken another approach.

Chapter Four

All That Jazz
Paris, France

Miranda was singing her last song for the night when someone caught her eye. In the rear of the club stood a gentleman that resembled Troy. She shook her head and continued to sing. To prove to herself that she was not going insane, she dared to look one more time. Their eyes met. *It is him.* She finished her song and looked again. He was gone.

She began to doubt what she thought she saw. It made no sense to her.

"What would Troy be doing in Paris and why in the heck would he be anywhere near me?"

Miranda walked over to Natalia. "You're not going to believe this, but I thought I saw Troy in the audience tonight."

Her friend raised her eyebrow and looked at Miranda as though she'd lost it. "Put the wine glass down. There is no way Troy is here." Natalia advised.

They both laughed, and Miranda waved it off. "You're right this glass of wine must be mighty strong."

Still in the back of her mind, she thought, "I didn't drink any wine before going on stage."

Two nights later, the same thing happened. This time Miranda was sure it was Troy. She looked him right in the eye. Natalia saw him as well and dropped the glass of water she was taking to a customer. Her mouth flew open. Miranda continued singing. She was nervous, but she kept singing anyway. When she finished she looked and once again Troy was gone.

After seeing Troy earlier tonight, all Miranda's insecurities from childhood returned. The feelings of abandonment. Her mother giving her up. Not feeling truly loved. The beatings she took at the various foster homes she was in. The questions returned. What did I do? She still had no closure where she and Troy were concerned.

When Troy left her, she felt emotionally drained. She knew she still loved him. She knew there was a physical attraction. What she did not know was if there was a God ordained connection between them? Something she should have made sure of before marrying him.

One night after she arrived home from the club, her telephone rang. It was Troy.

"Troy, how did you find me? Why are you here? Why now? Why did you leave me? Start
talking."

"I know you don't believe me, but I love you. I always have, I always will."

"Yeah right, Troy."

"Wait, just hear me out."

She didn't want to hear his explanations. Not now. She hung up.

The next night, Troy was waiting for her at the entrance of Jazz Fusion, the jazz theater and restaurant owned by Natalia. He started pleading his case. "Miranda, real men want to be able to provide for their woman. It was a man thing, I had to leave. I need you to understand this. Didn't you receive the money I sent you? I wanted to provide a life for you."

"Okay, Troy. I understand that, but what I don't understand is why you couldn't talk to me about the way you were feeling and what you were thinking about doing. We had already agreed that I would continue my dental practice while you pursue your music career, and once you were established, we would live off your salary while I pursued my music career. I needed more than your money, Troy. I needed you!"

Troy didn't say anything.

Miranda walked inside, leaving Troy outside. She wanted to slap the taste out of his mouth. Miranda stepped into Natalia's office and closed the door behind her, her body shaking. She gulped back the tears, "Troy was here. He was waiting outside."

Natalia stood and crossed the room to her friend. "Girl, what? How did he even know you were here? Where has he been? What has he been doing all this time? What could he possibly want? Why would he decide to show up just as you are putting your life back together?"

Natalia had too many questions. Miranda shrugged and held up her hands. She explained the best she could about what Troy had to say about his actions. After explaining, Miranda looked at her friend. "What do I do? I can't believe he did this to us. Why come back now?"

The next afternoon, Troy showed up at Jazz Fusion again. Apparently, he wanted to speak to Natalia, hoping that he could plead his case with Miranda's best friend. She invited him into her office, but held up her hand to stop him before he could talk.

"I know what you told Miranda. Troy, put yourself in her shoes for a minute. How would you like it if she disappeared on you? I bet you would have felt abandoned too. You were married and should have been able to talk to her about anything. You guys needed to make decisions together. That is what couples do. They work things out. Perhaps you could have been bi-coastal between Chicago and California. Maybe Miranda could have come to California on the weekend. Miranda could have moved to California and opened a dental practice there. You didn't give her the opportunity to choose any of those options because you just left her."

Troy rubbed his hand across his head. "You are right. I was a fool. A complete fool."

"You need to figure out how you are going to earn her trust again beginning with why after you left and even began to support her financially why you didn't pick up the telephone and call her."

Troy frowned, "I don't know why I didn't call her. I wanted to make everything perfect for her." His shoulders drooped. "I guess after a while I felt ashamed the way I left. I thought I was doing the right thing, but I see now I was selfish."

Natalia shook her head, "Good luck, buddy. I'm not helping you fix it and close the door on your way out."

Once Troy left, Natalia tried to return to her paperwork, instead she thought about the conversation she just had with Troy. She determined that Troy was a good man who didn't think things through. He made a mistake, a stupid unnecessary mistake. But Natalia knew how much her friend loved the man. Instead of going back to her work, she called Miranda.

Before Miranda finished her greeting, Natalia blurted, "Troy came by and I have to tell you he seems sincere. You two need to talk."

Miranda trusted Natalia's advice and agreed to meet with Troy. They went to a boulangerie for coffee and baguettes.

She didn't waste time, "I hear you talking, Troy, but can I trust you? Are you going to disappear again when the going gets tough? We should have been able to talk to one another about anything. Relationship – marriage, family, and friendships - equals communication, Troy. Marriage consists of give and take. The vows we took included for richer and for poorer. I don't know about you, but I took our vows seriously. I understand you wanted to be a man who could provide for his family, but you knew when we got married where you were at the time. And, I saw potential in you, otherwise I would not have agreed to pay most of the bills until you got your career on track. Lack of communication made a small problem a big, unnecessary problem. And here we are divorced because of it."

Troy leaned across the table, "I was young and dumb. I won't leave you again. I love you, Miranda. I write music for a major record company now. I can work from anywhere. I moved to Paris because I wanted to be with you. To love you, take care of you." He shook his head. "I won't give up, Miranda. I won't."

They talked some more while eating their meal. Miranda couldn't help but feel hopeful.

Over the next few weeks, Miranda found that Troy was indeed a big-time music writer. He wrote for many major music artists. He'd also written some songs for her and gave her the music. Miranda was impressed and agreed to perform the songs at the jazz theater restaurant. He was quite good, she had to admit. Troy made a habit of coming to the restaurant to eat dinner on the nights that Miranda performed. At first, this made her nervous, but she was getting used to him being around.

Troy called on the evening of her birthday to wish her happy birthday. When he called, she had been sniffing the beautiful flowers Troy sent her earlier in the day. She'd read the sweet card that came with the flowers over and over again while munching on the fabulous Parisian chocolates he sent as well.

My beloved Miranda,

Happy birthday to you. Would you do me the honor of letting me surprise you tonight and spend your birthday with me?

Love,

Troy

The flowers and chocolates were a pleasant surprise. Now Troy was asking her out on a date. She thought they were going to have another night of talking on the telephone. They had long talks that lasted through the night like they did when they first met. Only now they talked about things they should have talked about long ago before even considering marriage.

Since she had no plans for her birthday, she agreed to the date. Troy would not tell her where they were going. He just told her to dress in her fineries and to be ready at 7:00 pm.

Miranda was giddy. It had been a while since she'd been on a date. She dolled herself up to perfection, and when the doorbell rang took a quick look in the mirror pleased with what she saw.

Troy's eyes lit up. "Good evening, Miranda. You look stunning."

She blushed, "Why thank you, Troy. You look very handsome as usual."

They made small talk as Miranda tried to figure out where they were going. To her surprise, the driver pulled up in front of the Feerie. They went to see Moulin Rouge and had dinner. The show was fantastic, and the dinner was divine. The lobster was tender and juicy, and the asparagus was cooked to perfection. The expensive champagne went right to her head. The lights were low, and Miranda found herself loosening up a bit too much and determined the second glass of champagne was enough. Miranda enjoyed the cabaret. Although she didn't agree with the theme or the skimpy outfits that were a bit risqué for her taste, the music and dancing were exceptional, and she had a great time.

When they arrived at her home, she turned to Troy. "I was impressed tonight. Thank you for a wonderful evening."

Troy looked into her eyes, his brown eyes sparkled. "I want you to feel special, Miranda, and know how much I love you." He leaned in and gently kissed her on her lips.

She was getting weak but not yet ready to invite Troy in for fear of what would happen.

"Thank you again, Troy. Thank you for making my birthday celebration." This time she leaned in and kissed him. She turned to unlock her door. Inside, Miranda leaned against her door, still dazzled by the night.

Alone.

I'm really falling for him all over again.

A few nights later, Troy and Miranda had another date, this time at the Paris Jazz Festival. The performances were magnificent. When they got to Miranda's house after the festival, Troy walked Miranda to her door. "I would not have sought you out if I did not love you, Miranda."

Miranda stopped in her tracks but didn't turn around to face him. "Troy, when you left me, I felt abandoned, sad, confused, and wounded. I don't know if I can trust you. I know I am supposed to forgive, and I am trying very hard to do that, but how can I know you won't disappear again?"

Troy gently touched her shoulder. "Miranda, I promise I will never leave you or hurt you again. Please, trust me and give me another chance."

She took a deep breath and faced him. "I will call and make an appointment for us to meet with my pastor. If you are not willing to do that, there will be no us."

Troy nodded, "Text me and let me know the time of the meeting. I will be there with bells on."

Once inside her house, Miranda stood with her back pressed against the door as the words she so desperately wanted to hear flowed into her like a healing balm.

Chapter Five

Reunited

Miranda made the necessary calls to her pastor's secretary to make an appointment for herself and Troy to meet for counseling. To her surprise, Troy showed up for all the meetings and consultations. Miranda's pastor began the first session by referring to their wedding vows, particularly the for richer and poorer part and she had not even told him what the problem was in the marriage. The only thing he knew was they were divorced, considering remarrying and needed to work on some things.

During their last session, her pastor recommended a weekend couples retreat. Miranda was surprised by the number of couples in attendance. She felt better knowing it was not just her and Troy that wanted to work at bettering their relationship. Everyone seemed opened to sharing about their difficulties and trying to improve. All the couples were willing to participate in the projects and exercises the group leaders had planned for them.

After they returned, Miranda commented, "I enjoyed the retreat. I think it was a success."

Troy reached for her, "I agree I think we should attend annually I learned a lot. It will keep our relationship fresh."

His comments made Miranda smile and joy filled her heart. After the sessions with the pastor and retreat, she was seriously considering taking Troy back. She figured why meet a new nut and start all over trying to build a relationship with someone. She already knew Troy well. She knew his good qualities and his shortcomings. She just had to be sure they kept the communication line open if she decided to remarry him.

Troy began to attend church with her. One Sunday morning, he walked to the front of the church and joined as the doors of the church were opened for membership. She never pressured him, but she was delighted he had made this decision on his own.

The theater was packed tonight. The lights were low. The spotlight was on Miranda. She was glowing as she sang like a songbird. Her audience was captivated as they listened to her perform. Little did she know; a major music mogul was in the audience. Unbeknownst to her, Troy had sent a copy of her tape along with a media kit to the record company he worked with. After her performance, the music mogul walked up and introduced himself.

He praised her performance and expressed an interest in signing her. They offered her an astronomical amount of money, a grand house back in the States and many benefits, but Miranda was not interested. She preferred performing in the small intimate jazz café. Many years ago, Miranda would have jumped and leaped for joy at this opportunity, and she was flattered but now all she wanted was simplicity, comfort, and love.

It was their date night and Troy took Miranda for dinner in the Eiffel Tower. Although she had been to the

58 Tour Eiffel restaurant on the first floor on many occasions, she had yet to go to the famed Michelin three-star restaurant Le Jules Verne on the top floor of the Eiffel tower.

Miranda was completely delighted. The restaurant was amazing, and the cuisine itself was an experience. The ambience was perfect for a romantic evening. The sun was going down and the city of lights was all aglow.

When they finished dinner and desert, Troy got on one knee and proposed to her. She said yes. They left the restaurant hand in hand and went to purchase a lock. At the famous Pont des Arts, a bridge that couples placed locks on and threw away the key as a symbol of love and luck, Miranda and Troy affixed their lock to the love lock bridge. Miranda would always remember this night.

After a year of counseling and courtship, Miranda and Troy, along with Natalia, began to plan a big fancy wedding. They did not rush. They learned the hard way that fools rush in. Natalia helped Miranda pick out her wedding gown and assisted with anything else that needed to be done for the wedding. She offered her jazz club and restaurant for the reception venue, free of charge. She also insisted on providing the food and drinks.

Troy gave up his small apartment and moved into Miranda's house. They came to an agreement that words were of utmost importance. God spoke words, and they needed to speak words and communicate since God resides in them. The couple was remarried and included in

their vows, 'the line of communication is key and will always be open in our marriage.'

On the day of the wedding, before the ceremony took place, Troy advised Miranda that he had invited a special guest. Miranda noticed an unfamiliar face in the seat next to Troy's mother, but the lady looked familiar. A young lady and a young man that looked like the lady accompanied her. Miranda looked again, the lady looked like her.

"Oh my God! Mommy!"

Troy had found her mother, and she also had a sister and a brother that strongly resemble her. Miranda ran up to her mother and they hugged for what seemed like a lifetime. Her mother tried to explain what happened, but Miranda shook her head. All she wanted was to savor the moment, they would talk about it later.

They finally parted so that the wedding ceremony could be performed. This was the best wedding present Troy could have given her. She had a family. Her own family, and Miranda was filled with joy.

Miranda and Troy traveled back and forth between Paris and California. Paris was their home base. Periodically, Troy had to go to California for business meetings, music award shows and guest appearances. And, the lovely Miranda was never far from his side.

She visited her mom, sister and brother while Troy was working. And she loved when her family came to Paris to visit her. She had a host of nieces and nephew running around the house spreading joy. Miranda felt loved and comforted. The nieces and nephews gave her practice for Troy, Jr. that she was carrying around in her stomach.

Merci Beaucoup!

About the Author

Annie M. Johnson has enjoyed reading since a very early age. She remembered joking and saying often after reading books, "I can do that, I can write a book." Her first book titled *Favor* was published in 2005. Since then, she has written and published *Holiday Mayhem*, *Survivor Seduction Aboard the SS Sunshine*, and *Life's Song a Miracle*. *Torn* was published with Peace in The Storm Publishing. *Powerful Woman Where Does Your Power Come From?* was published with Imani Faith Publishing.

Southern Delights
Tyora Moody

1

I'd taken a few days off from the day job where I worked as a public relations manager. I loved my job, but I longed for the day when I could write full-time. Not that I didn't do a lot of writing for my day job, I was constantly writing press releases and copy for my company's social media platforms and blog. And while I was not a believer in writer's block, I couldn't find time to write my next book no matter how hard I tried.

My editor had been harassing me the past month and had already extended the deadline for another six months. So, this week, I was determined to nail down a few chapters. With two books under my belt, I was still tickled to see my name, Nia Michaels, on a book cover. Crazy thing was, I wrote sweet romance novels that weren't anything like my life.

Maybe that's my problem. I need romance in my own life. Sigh!

Lately, I'd been in a funk. Three years had passed since I'd been in a serious relationship, and let's just say the last one turned me off to the whole dating, boyfriend process. That's what it was to me, a process to see if I was a good match for someone else. I wasn't having much success. My constant prayer was to be ready for when Mr. Right would find me.

Lord, I'm wondering if I'm even showing up on the GPS.

After my last break up, I received the inspiration to write a novel. I'd always wanted to write a book, and I'm not certain if it was just the right time or whether it was due to me not wanting to be depressed, but I wrote a whole book. Sebastian Windsor, the male character from *Sugar & Spice* was indeed the man of my dreams. I wanted to marry Sebastian myself by the time I typed the end. Then, I proceeded to write another book, *Sweet on You*, with yet another male character that I wished was real. Avery Vance was his name. What can I tell you? I'm good at writing the perfect man. My readers agree with me because both books have had relatively good success. I enjoy visiting with book clubs to talk about my stories. For the past year, those same readers have been hounding me on social media wanting to know when to expect my next book.

I sighed for like the fifth time since I entered Southern Delights Cafe, a coffee shop owned by my aunt Linda. I wasn't sure what was going on with book number three, but I was anxious for something to spark my imagination. When I arrived, my aunt took one look at me and fixed my favorite, a caramel mocha latte on the house. I guess she could tell from my face, it was one of those kind of days.

I'd been sitting in a back booth for close to forty minutes, positioned where I could see the lunch crowd walk through the door. By now, a whole lot of customers had ventured inside to grab a cup of their favorite coffee beverage, usually paired with one of Aunt Linda's sweet treats. I finished nibbling on a mini pecan pie only to find a blank page still staring back at me. I drained my cup and thought about trying another sugary delight. What I needed was for my brain cells to focus on my laptop instead of obsessing over the dessert counter. My bottom sure didn't need the extra calories. My jeans were fitting way too snug, and I was basically wasting away my gym membership.

While I struggled with temptation, a figure caught my eye outside the cafe. I'm not sure why, but I found my eyes roving from the dessert counter to outside the window. Maybe it was

the beautiful chocolate skin or the strong jawline visible from the side that captured my attention. When the man reached for the door, I sat still, almost not breathing and watched as the most gorgeous man I'd seen in a long, long time walked through the doors. He had a bit of swagger to his walk as he glided towards the order counter.

For a brief moment, he turned and caught my eye.
I smiled.
He smiled back.
It crossed my mind that I must have looked quite silly gaping at him. Yeah, I was pretty sure, my mouth had fell open at some point. He actually smiled at me. Me. To save myself, I turned my attention back to my laptop determined to look like I was busy. I even started typing on the keyboard. What I was typing, I don't know. I just knew my body had grown warm despite the cool flow of air in the cafe.

My aunt Linda was usually in the back pulling fresh baked goods out of her oven, but she must have given her barista a break. I heard her voice ask, "What can I get for you, sir?"

I cocked my ear to the side so I could hear his voice, and what a melodious voice it was. Deep and smooth with a southern drawl. "I will have a Cafe Americano."

Mr. Cafe Americano knew his coffee. It was mid-afternoon and his espresso selection would definitely be the perfect perk-me up. I could almost hear the smile in my aunt Linda's voice without even turning around. "It will be right up. Would you like anything to go with that today?"

I took that moment to turn my attention towards the dessert counter, this time my focus on the goods outside the glass counter. *Lord, help me.* Mr. Cafe Americano's back was to me, but I could tell he was a man who probably worked out. His muscles weren't bulging, but his crisp white button-down shirt stretched over broad shoulders. I observed as he stepped over to the dessert counter to peruse the sweet treats behind the glass.

Southern Delights Cafe was known for their southern baked goods as much as their coffee. Aunt Linda's specialties were her pies which often included pecan pie, sweet potato pie, peach cobbler and apple pie. Lately, she'd been experimenting with mini-pies.

I heard tapping from the left and swiveled my head to catch my aunt eying me with a mischievous smile on her face. Ugh! I'd been caught gawking at her customer. Knowing my aunt, she was not going to let that slide. She knew I couldn't help it. Aunt Linda was over fifty, but she'd been quite the catch in her day. Age had calmed her down, along with Jesus, but she had no qualms with checking out a good-looking man.

I could almost hear her favorite saying, "Girl, God gave us eyes to see with."

There was no arguing with my auntie about the part of the bible that mentioned "lust of the eyes" was not a good thing. I took a deep breath to cleanse my mind and refocused on my laptop. I read the gibberish I typed.

Mocha colored brother. Swagger for days. Deep, smooth voice.

Seriously, that's what I typed?

The more I looked at the words, the more I thought this wasn't a bad thing. This guy, Mr. Cafe Americano, was the *perfect* male interest for my novel. Inspiration had finally arrived. From the side of my eye, I noticed the man who'd now become a character in my book was eagerly pointing to a tray of freshly baked mini apple pies. When he spoke, my ears perked up.

"I definitely want to try one of those."

My aunt Linda asked, "Would you like me to heat it up for you?"

"That would be great."

A minute later, I heard my aunt call my name. I turned to look at her. She stood grinning and holding up a silver carafe. "Nia, you look like you're hard at work over there. You want a refill?"

The man turned around and looked at me, his white smile dazzling.

If I could have disappeared at that moment, I would have. I tried not show a grimace on my face. "Sure, I could use some more coffee." I scooted out of the booth, suddenly feeling shy. Wearing my purple t-shirt emblazoned with "I'm Blessed" in large white letters on the front and my favorite jeans, which were not too shabby but definitely fitted, I believed in being comfortable. I hadn't come dressed to impress.

I tried to not look at Mr. Cafe Americano, but sensed him checking me out. I walked over to the counter and handed my aunt my empty cup.

She gave me a sly smile. "You like the view today?"

I rolled my eyes. Even though it was a bright and sunny day, I knew she wasn't talking about outside. Southern Delights Cafe was located in the heart of downtown Charlotte, so the views around us were tall buildings and people bustling up and down the sidewalk. A decent view for a writer looking for inspiration within a metropolitan setting. But today, inspiration had walked through the door and was patiently waiting beside me.

I murmured thanks to my aunt as she passed my refilled cup. She winked at me, knowing she had me all flustered. I felt like I was walking like some old woman on the way back to my booth, fearing I would do something foolish like trip and spill my coffee. As soon as the thought entered my mind, I paused in the middle of my walk, willing myself to forget the thought.

To my right, a voice interrupted my brief trance. Stunned, I turned to catch Mr. Cafe Americano smiling at me.

He really was gorgeous!

"Looks like you're hard at work over there," he said. "I can imagine you needed that shot of caffeine pretty badly."

I smiled back, "This time of day? Yes, it's a bit of a struggle."

He nodded, "Oh, I know the feeling. I like to come here to get a quick pick me up for the afternoon. Today has been especially rough at work."

I wanted to ask him where he worked. Had to be nearby since he walked over. Once folks around here parked their cars in the nearby garages, they usually didn't move them until rush hour in the evening.

My aunt said, "Your order is ready. Enjoy."

I observed his well-manicured fingers as he reached for his cup and bag. He winked at my aunt, "Thank you, ma'am."

He seems like a bit of a flirt.

The thought sobered me, and I headed back to my booth. But before he left out, Mr. Cafe Americano turned and waved. "Nice talking to you. I hope the rest of your day is blessed."

"You too," I waved back, and then watched him walk down the sidewalk as far as I could see out the window.

My aunt guffawed. "Girl, if you lean over any farther, you will fall out that booth."

I straightened my back, ignoring my aunt's laughter. I was glad there wasn't many other customers inside the cafe to witness my embarrassment.

A few seconds later, my aunt appeared at my booth and sat down. "What have you been working on all this time?"

"My new novel. By the way, you didn't have to embarrass me. I was just checking out the guy. He's actually perfect as my character."

"Mmm. He's also perfect for other things too. He seemed interested."

I looked at my aunt as if she'd grown something on her nose. "Seriously, I'm pretty sure I will never see him again."

"Oh I don't know. He's a regular."

That piqued my interest. "Really?"

"So you are interested?"

"No."

"Girl, stop playing. It's been too long. I have always told you God has someone for you, but you have to be open to the possibilities."

"I am open. He seemed nice." I squinted my eyes, "Did you have to call my name out like that?"

My aunt laughed, "How else was I supposed to get your attention? You were staring. Which is rude, *by the way.*"

I couldn't help it.

"Whatever! I need to get back to work. I appreciate the free coffee today. Thank you, Auntie."

"Mmmm, I hope it's helping. I've been waiting on a new book from you. You seem to have been on hold for some reason. It's time to wake up."

"That's what I'm doing, Auntie."

Once my aunt left me alone, I began tapping away on the keyboard and before I knew it I had a very rough, but deeply satisfying first chapter.

To keep the story flowing though, maybe I should return. I wouldn't mind meeting Mr. Cafe Americano again.

2

The next few weeks were super busy at work. The story was flowing and I wrote whenever I had a chance, usually during my lunch break and at night before bedtime. When I wrote at night, I would write to the early morning hours. I wasn't a morning person so the late nights didn't help. I stopped by Southern Delights Cafe mainly in the morning to grab a cup of coffee and some breakfast quiche. Aunt Linda served bacon and cheese or sausage and cheese quiches to the morning crowd.

My aunt amazed me with the amount of baking she did. She was always in the kitchen Monday through Friday. Since her business was located downtown and pretty busy throughout the week, she kept the cafe closed on the weekends. The baking didn't stop though.

One particular Saturday, my aunt was preparing desserts for an afternoon program at Victory Gospel Church. My family has been a part of this congregation since I was a child. Now as an adult out on my own, I still attended with my mom each Sunday. I was the youngest of three, but my older sister and brother both moved away after graduating high school. Even though I was the only sibling who remained near my mother in Charlotte, I had my own place. My dad had passed away about five years ago from a heart attack, and my aunt Linda moved in with my mom and took over my old room.

When Aunt Linda required some help baking, she could always count on her older sister to help. Usually, between the two women, I would get roped into helping too. That was how I found myself armed with my laptop on my mom's couch trying to add to my word count before I was held hostage in the kitchen.

My mom walked through and kissed me on my head. "You getting some writing done today?"

"Yes, I have to get this book finished."

Mom smiled at me, "You can do it. I know you can."

Aunt Linda came through the living room, dressed with an apron that was already covered in flour. "Are you two going to leave me hanging today?"

Mom narrowed her eyes at her younger sister, "Linda, let Nia work on her book. We can handle the baking today."

Linda looked over at me. "Oh, I forgot. Speaking of your book, you missed your man yesterday."

I blurted, "What? When?"

My mom swung her head back and forth between me and my aunt. "What man?"

Linda grinned and slapped her hand on her apron, sending flour dust into the air. "A few weeks ago, this handsome young man came to Southern Delights and took your daughter's breath away. He is gorgeous, the kind that makes a girl trip over herself. Also quite the gentleman."

I eyed my aunt. "I didn't trip."

Linda waved her finger, "No ... but you definitely got his attention. He asked about you."

She had my attention. I swiveled on the couch to stare at her, my laptop forgotten. "What do you mean?"

My aunt rubbed her hands together as if she had something really good to tell me. Her grin reminded me of Cheshire Cat in *Alice in Wonderland*. "He asked if I knew the woman that was sitting with the laptop that day. I told him you were my niece."

I jumped up from the couch. "No, you didn't. What else did you do?"

Linda rolled her eyes. "Well, I didn't give him your number if that's what you're worried about. He's a regular; I see him all the time. In fact, I believe his first name is Brendan..." She placed her hand under her chin, deep in thought. "No, maybe it's Brandon ... something like that. So many people come through the café, and we try to write their names on their coffee cups, but the names start to blend together..."

I cut off my aunt's rambling. "Okay, so that's all you know about him? Does he work nearby?"

My mom frowned at me. "Why are you asking her? What are you planning to do?"

I sighed, "Nothing. Look, Mom, I learned my lesson the last time. You said don't go chasing after a man."

"That's right." Mom exclaimed, "It says in Proverbs, 'He who finds a wife finds what is good and receives favor from the LORD.' Mom placed her hands on her hip and stared at me.

Mom knew how much my last boyfriend had upset me. She warned me then not to go chasing after the business executive who liked to travel. I decided to chase after him, surprise him while he was away, and showed up at his Atlanta hotel I learned the hard way that he often had a woman for company during his travels.

The surprise was on me.

Aunt Linda swatted at my mom, "Your daughter is just curious about the man. Their connection was really obvious even in that short time. He's obviously been thinking about her." My aunt narrowed her eyes. "If I'm not mistaken, you must have been thinking about him too."

I wasn't about to admit to my mom and aunt that every single time I worked on my manuscript, and even when I wasn't writing, I thought about Mr. Cafe

Americano. I sighed, "He was just a gentleman. You don't see that these days."

My aunt winked at me, "No, you don't. Not in young men like him. I will see what else I can dig up on him. I can tell you he usually comes into the cafe mid-afternoon. Not every day, but at least once or twice a week."

I grinned at my aunt. "Is this your way of encouraging me to be there when he shows up?"

With a raised eyebrow, her grin conspiratorial, "It wouldn't hurt."

The problem with my aunt's idea is I worked a few miles from Southern Delights. It wouldn't be easy for me to swing by her cafe and then get back to work on a lunch hour. The days I swung by to grab coffee and breakfast, I was almost always late getting into the office. I would have to figure out if I could take a day off, but when that would be, I didn't know since we had some big projects launching this month.

Would I ever meet Mr. Cafe Americano again in person? Or would I have to settle with the version my imagination had cooked up for my novel?

3

Severe thunderstorms warnings had threatened all day. It was late June and summer storms were a normal part of being in the South. By the time I left work, the rain was pouring so hard, I decided I would just wait out the storm. I knew I didn't want to waste valuable time sitting in traffic; today was already turning into a bust. I managed to forget my umbrella and got my clothes wet and my hair as well, thanks to the whipping wind.

When I arrived at Southern Delights, my aunt wasn't visible in the front. I walked up to the barista working today, Kelley Long. She was my aunt's longest working barista, a little bit older than most of the college age workers.

Kelley greeted me warmly, "It's a mess out there today. What can I get for you?"

"Just coffee today." I needed hot liquid to warm me back up and decided to keep it simple.

I grabbed the coffee and added two sugars and cream, pleased to see not many customers hiding from the rain. My favorite booth was open. I pulled out my laptop and sipped the warm liquid, waiting for my laptop to boot. Once I opened my manuscript, my fingers connected to the keyboard. I was able to zone out my surroundings and enter the world of my characters. So enthralled by my own writing, I hadn't noticed others had decided to hide out in the cafe anyway. I glimpsed a growing line of rain-soaked stragglers inching towards the counter. My aunt was out front now with her baristas taking care of orders as fast as they were called out.

While my head was turned, someone had stopped near my table. I looked up into the beautiful brown eyes of Mr. Cafe Americano or whatever his name was.

He smiled, "Hello, I see we had the same idea."

My face grew warm as I reached for my laptop and closed it. I'd only been writing about the man, as a fictional character, of course. Now, he was standing in front of me. "Yeah," I stammered, "I have been caught in traffic with these storms before. Not fun, but it should pass in the next hour or so." My eyes swept the cafe, noticing most of the booths had been filled. I gulped as I looked back at him. I couldn't believe what I was about to do, but I offered, "Would you like to sit?"

He raised an eyebrow. "Are you sure? You seemed pretty deep in your work."

I waved as if it was nothing. "I could use a break."

He slid into the booth in front of me. I tried to suck in a breath, but my chest felt tight all of a sudden like the breath had been knocked out of me.

Why was I reacting like this? I was a grown woman, not some teenager.

I glanced at the counter. My aunt didn't seem to notice I was there today, which was probably a good thing. She would have caused me to freak out even more.

I turned back to Mr. Cafe Americano and smiled. *It sure would be nice to know his name.* I held out my hand, "I'm Nia Michaels."

Taking my hand in his, he grinned. "The author?"

I frowned. He didn't strike me as one who read romance novels. "How did you know?"

He winked. "Your aunt mentioned it to me."

"Oh." I nodded. *Thanks, Auntie.* "You are?"

"Brendan McCormick."

Finally... a name. Then, I noticed he was still holding my hand. He had really nice hands. I pulled my hand back and placed them both in my lap, suddenly aware of my wet clothes sticking to me. I reached up and raked my fingers through my hair, which I'd recently had cut down shorter. On most days, I kept it smooth around the side with curls on top. The way my hair was drooping on my forehead, I was sure those curls had become a mass of messiness.

I looked back at him. "Do you work around here?"

"I do, two streets over. I work as a financial advisor at Nobles Finance."

"Wow, you trekked all the way over here? You're brave to walk in this rain."

He smiled, "I like the walk. And Southern Delights definitely offers the best coffee around town, not to mention, I love pie. In fact, I'm thinking about buying a full pie for next weekend. Some good friends invited me to their home and I thought it be best not to arrive empty-handed."

I chuckled. "That's thoughtful of you. You're going to make someone really happy with one of my aunt's pies."

"Do you cook too?"

I shrugged. "Not the way my mom and aunt cook, but I do alright."

He grinned, "I'm not too bad myself."

I raised an eyebrow. "Really?"

His smile was shy, reflective. "I learned from the best. You're lucky the women in your life are still around. In the kitchen, I feel closest to the women who are no longer here like my mom and grandma. Those women believed in cooking old fashioned Southern meals and had no problem preparing for armies of people. I only have to cook for one, but I like to play around with..." he made quotes with his fingers, "... healthier versions of the food they cooked."

"I'm sorry about your losses." He was right, I was lucky. Even though my mom and her sister could be a pain sometimes, I didn't know what I would do without them. I cocked my head to the side, "So you like to experiment with cooking healthy foods. Sounds like the makings of a real chef."

His eyes locked on me. "In a past life, I would have loved to be a chef."

I mulled over his revelation, feeling incredible with how much he revealed about himself in a few minutes. We sipped our coffee. Mine had grown cold, but I didn't mind. The rain outside was still pouring down as if it would never let up. I was in good company and had nowhere in particular to be... other than getting back to my writing.

I can wait out the storm a bit longer. This is good research for my character, I thought to myself.

Brendan spoke first, breaking our silence, which hadn't really been that awkward. I was surprised with how comfortable I felt around him so quickly. The image I had of him had been in my head for weeks now. The real man, Brendan McCormick was a treat to behold.

"So what sparked your interest in writing? "

I got this question all the time, but I didn't want to tell him my interest in writing was sparked by a bad relationship. Instead, I told him, "I have always enjoyed creative writing. I do have a day job, mainly writing press releases, blogs and social media copy. Not the most exciting stuff to write. A few years ago, I started on a story and it grew into a novel. I pitched it to an agent at a conference, and the rest is history."

"That's awesome. I've thought about writing a book. I've even jotted down some ideas."

I leaned forward in the booth. "I highly recommend joining a writers' group or attending a writers' conference. It helps to have the support and learn about the craft."

"Any recommendations?"

Recommendations? I tried not to make my grin too wide since I saw the possibilities of his question. "I can send some resources and links to you."

"Sure, let me give you my card." Brendan pulled a business card out of his jacket pocket that had the Nobles Finance logo on the front. Then, he pulled out a navy blue pen with the same logo.

Well, his day job is legit.

I watched as he jotted a phone number on the back, then on the next line, his email address. "Here you go. If you wouldn't mind emailing me, I'd appreciate it."

I stared at the card. My eyes were more on his number, my thoughts wondering why he'd shared it. I nodded, "I will email you soon."

"Great. I look forward to seeing you again. Soon, I hope."

"Sounds like a plan."

Brendan slid out of the booth, not taking his eyes off me. "Have a good night, Nia."

"You too, Brendan." I waved slightly, feeling all the comfort and warmth from the past few minutes slip away. I'm not sure why my nervousness returned after he left the booth, but I peered down at my hand, my eyes zoning in on his phone number.

Did he want me to call him too?

"What you got there?"

I jumped in the seat, clutching my chest. I turned to stare at my aunt. "Where did you come from?"

My aunt frowned at me. "Uhm, child I know your head is all messed up from having that good looking man sitting with you, but you do remember I own this place?"

I blinked, wondering why my favorite spot happened to be owned by my family. Nosy family at that. "Brendan gave me his information. I'm going to send him some recommendations since he's interested in writing."

My aunt slid into the space Brendan had just occupied. "Well, aren't you Miss Smartie? Got a name and some contact information. I'm proud of you."

I rolled my eyes and chuckled at my aunt's silliness. Aunt Linda did have a point. Instead of a bust, today turned out to be a blessing. I had a way to reach out to Brendan McCormick.

4

I gathered the writers' resources and emailed them to Brendan. Then, I waited. I mean I wasn't waiting around not doing anything. Life went on, but I'd emailed him on a Saturday morning and he responded Monday evening. The moment I saw his email in my inbox, it was like the world stopped. It was a short email, and I can't remember the number of times I read it. Somehow, I found myself in a loop of reading it over and over again like it was a love letter or something.

Thank you, Nia. I know as an author you must be pretty busy with your writing so I appreciate you sharing these resources. I really do hope we can meet again. I enjoy talking to you and feel like we would make great friends.

Make great friends. It definitely wasn't a love letter.

I wasn't sure what to think about the last line. I had the man's phone number, I could just call him. While I was a modern woman, I felt really apprehensive about just calling Brendan out of the blue. Wouldn't I seem desperate? I mean he indicated he was looking for friendship. Which in fact, was what I wanted to. I didn't want to fall head over heels for someone only to be disappointed. I wanted to get to know the man.

I debated how to respond back to Brendan's email for the rest of the week. I even considered emailing him my phone number. Let him be the one to call.

By the time the weekend rolled around, my enthusiasm about Brendan had turned to anxiety. I was feeling more like I had blown an opportunity.

One of my best friends, Angel Cade, had invited me to her son's first birthday party. I sometimes babysat for the little tyke and was excited to see him reach this milestone. Back in the day, before Angel met the love of her life, Wes Cade, we used to hang out more often. Me, Angel and my other best friend, Toni Reed, were quite the threesome in high school. Now, both my BFFs had men. Toni was engaged with a wedding planned later this summer. I was happy for both of them that their Mr. Right had found them. I prayed one day I would experience the same reality. In the meantime, I guess I would settle with writing the perfect romance novel.

I'd come along quite nicely, finishing my first draft. I took a much needed break which meant I wasn't visiting Southern Delights as often. I usually only visited the coffeehouse for inspiration. The down and dirty of rewriting I reserved for when I was rested and had a bit more quiet time on the weekend. I was determined to send the editor something she would love. *Matters of the Heart* would be published next spring, and that was something to be excited about.

When I arrived at the Cade's house, barbecue smells wafted enticing my nose. While this was clearly a toddler's birthday party, there were probably more adults at the house than children. As I made my way to the kitchen, I counted at least six children of varying ages. The only toddler in the bunch was Wes, Jr. who was in full force, giggling and pumping his little legs. He plowed right into me.

I reached down and picked up the little boy, "Happy birthday to you. You're a happy little boy today, aren't you?" I held him on my hip and walked back towards the kitchen.

Angel met me at the door, "Thank you for catching him. He's wide open today and believe it or not, he hasn't had any sugar yet."

I laughed, "Wow. Well, at least he will sleep good tonight." I handed Wes, Jr., who had started squirming, to his mother.

"I hope so." Angel grabbed her son, "Thanks for coming to help. I haven't heard from you since you've been in your writing cave. Are you finished?"

"Yes, I have a pretty decent rough draft. I decided to put it to the side today and actually do something social. So, how can I help?"

Angel turned, "Folks have been bringing dishes, which I appreciate, but I'm running out of room for them. Wes set up a table outside. I was thinking any food that would be okay outside, we can put on the table."

"Sure, I can handle that."

It took some maneuvering through the back door which seemed like a revolving door as children ran in and out. Wes strolled through carrying meat from the grill.

"Good to see you, Nia. Hey, I have someone for you to meet when you get a moment."

"Oh, okay." I hoped Wes wasn't about to embark on a matchmaking venture. Everyone around me had tried to be a matchmaker.

Please don't, people! Let a sister enjoy her singleness.

I arranged most of the dishes and was making sure there was enough serving utensils when I heard my name. At first, my mind felt confused.

I know that voice.

I turned and almost dropped the spoon in my hand. In what could only be described as a juggling act, I managed to not let the spoon hit the ground. I looked up to catch Brendan grinning at me.

He nodded his head, "Nice move. Sorry to scare you."

"No, it's fine. I wasn't, um, expecting you."

"I was a little surprised to see you too." He handed me a familiar brown bag with handles and the Southern Delights logo on the side.

I exclaimed, "You brought the pie for Wes, Jr.'s birthday party."

"Yeah, I knew Wes and Angel are fans of your aunt's pies. They introduced me to the apple pie."

"Oh." I reached inside the bag and took out the pie, sitting it alongside the banana pudding. "How do you know Wes and Angel?"

"I went to school with Wes. We were roommates."

"Really? Wow, small world. Angel is one of my oldest friends. We graduated from the same high school."

We stared at each other for I don't know how long. I was still a bit amazed to see him in person. I guess he was too. We'd only met inside of Southern Delights. He looked good, as usual, but today he was dressed down wearing jeans, a polo shirt and sneakers.

Is there anything this man doesn't look good wearing?

Once again, I was self-conscious about what I was wearing. Thank goodness, I decided to wear a golden yellow sundress and sandals. The humidity was in full blast, so I could only hope my hair was still holding the style.

Behind me, I heard high-pitched shrieks and turned to see what looked like an army of children, but really only the few in attendance, stampede towards us. Why the excitement I didn't know, but I felt Brendan's hand on my arm. He maneuvered me out of the way just as the young'uns sprinted past us.

I placed my hand on my chest to calm my beating heart. "What was that about?"

Brendan laughed, "Wes just called out it's time to eat. I guess they were hungry."

"You'd think no has fed them for days the way they tore towards that door."

"Why don't we grab a plate too?"

That sounded like a plan to me. We balanced heavy paper plates back towards a corner of the patio. In between eating, Brendan regaled me with college stories of him and Wes. Once again, I was pleasantly surprised with how comfortable I felt eating and talking with him. I could count the number of times I'd seen Brendan in person on one hand, but I felt like I'd known him a long time.

After most folks left, I helped Angel clean the kitchen while she put the birthday boy to bed. Brendan stopped in the kitchen, and without asking, he grabbed a dish towel and began drying dishes.

I commented, "This was fun."

He nodded, "It was. I wanted to thank you again for sending me the writers' resources. You had quite a list."

"I hope it wasn't too overwhelming."

"No, I appreciate it." He finished drying a serving dish and placed it on the counter. "I was kind of hoping you would call."

I paused with my hands deep in the sudsy water. "You did give me your phone number, but I wasn't sure. I know I should be the modern woman and know it's okay to call a guy, still..."

He stepped up to the sink and raised his eyebrow. "That's okay. Maybe you can share your number with me?"

I had no issue with that. I took my hands out of the water and reached for dish towel to dry them. "I can call you so you can add my number to your contacts." While I hadn't called him, I still had his business card tucked in the pocket of my phone holder.

Brendan's phone rang after I dialed. He answered while looking at me and grinned, "Got it."

I put my phone away as he tapped in my information.

He looked up after tucking his phone in his back pocket. "Since it seems we keep meeting each other, how about we go out on a real date?"

"That would be nice... Just as long as it's not at my aunt's coffeehouse," I teased.

He threw his head back and laughed. "I believe I can do better than that. I got the feeling your aunt would want me to take you someplace else anyway. How about dinner next Friday?"

This was actually happening! I couldn't have wrote a scene like this if I tried.

I beamed, "Dinner would be nice."

5

It had been awhile since I went out on a date. I forgot the anxiety I went through with picking out an outfit. By the time I settled on one of my favorite outfits, a pink short-sleeved blouse and a long flowery skirt, I was hoping not to collapse due to my nerves. I was beyond butterflies in my stomach, but something was doing somersaults and making me shaky. I also hadn't eaten much today, and I was sure that didn't help. But I didn't know why I was reacting this way. I'd seen Brendan on a number of occasions, and each time, he displayed interest. And I felt so comfortable around him.

That's what worried me. This week, I'd managed to make myself paranoid. My thoughts were that maybe Brendan was too good to be true.

Trust in the LORD with all your heart and lean not on your own understanding; in all your ways submit to him, and he will make your paths straight.

I kept this Bible verse plastered to my bathroom mirror. Seems like a strange place to put a Bible verse but reading Proverbs 3:5-6 had a calming effect on me.

I shut my eyes. *Lord, I don't believe Brendan has shown up in my life for no reason. I believe you meant for us to meet and become friends. Whatever comes after that, I will trust you.*

That was my problem in the past, I pushed ahead. I needed to continue to wait and see where God intended for this budding relationship to go.

I'd chosen to meet Brendan at Maggiano's Italian Restaurant. One glance at the clock by my bed made me realize I needed to leave in the next ten minutes. As I traveled down I-77, I could feel my body slowly becoming more relaxed.

I found a parking space at the SouthPark Mall, and to my pleasant surprise, Brendan was standing outside Maggiano's, glancing down at his phone. He must have sensed I was walking towards him because he lifted his head and turned on that bright smile. All the unease I felt seemed to have been replaced by giddiness.

I smiled back, "Hopefully, you weren't waiting too long?"

"No, not at all. You're right on time." He held out his arm towards me. "Shall we head inside?"

I hooked my arm into his, drawing comfort in how well my arm nestled inside of his. Once inside, we were quickly seated near a window.

I ordered the four cheese ravioli, while Brendan opted for the baked ziti. We chatted a bit, but we both must have been famished, savoring our dishes in comfortable silence. The waiter inquired about dessert, and somehow Brendan talked me into ordering. He didn't have to do too much convincing.

I wasn't ready for the date to end.

We both ended up with New York Style cheesecake, and while we consumed dessert, he asked, "You write romance novels. Do you believe in love at first sight?"

His question stunned me. I swallowed before responding, "I believe that people know when they've met the right person."

He agreed and sat back, "I think so too. I have to admit that I stopped dating for a while. It seemed kind of pointless."

I know my mouth fell open. "You too?"

He snickered, "I take it you took a break too?"

I sighed, "I wanted to be around someone I felt comfortable with, someone I felt was committed to see where the relationship would go."

He laid his fork down and wiped his mouth before looking at me. "God has perfect timing. I believe we want the same thing. I want to get to know you better, Nia. If you are okay with it, I'd like to ask you out again."

I wiped my own mouth, hoping to control the goofy grin that had taken over my face. "I look forward to getting to know you, Brendan."

We walked out of Maggiano's, and this time Brendan held my hand as he walked me to my car. He peered down at me, "Next time, I'd like to make dinner for you."

I grinned, "That sounds like a plan, Chef. How about I bring our favorite apple pie?"

"Perfect. I'm looking forward to it. Next Saturday?"

"It's a date."

"Great," he smiled back at me.

Before I climbed into my car, Brendan reached down and placed a gentle kiss on my cheek.

As I headed back home, my cheek warmed from the kiss. I thought about Brendan's question. *Do you believe in love at first sight?*

Deep down, I knew he was the one I'd been waiting for, possibly from the first time I saw him inside Southern Delights. He wasn't a man created from my imagination, but I believed God ordered our paths to cross at just the right time.

This week my mind wasn't filled with unnecessary doubts. Brendan called me, and a few nights, I called him. We talked every night for hours. I teased him on

Friday night, "So, what can I expect from the chef tomorrow?"

Brendan's voice had dropped like he was about to share a great secret. "It's a surprise, but I know you will love it."

"You're very confident."

He chuckled. "I have made this meal a few times. It's one of the first meals I experimented with when I started cooking seriously."

"Well, I can't wait."

Saturday morning, I read my draft of *Matters of the Heart* for the last time before emailing the document to my editor. I knew the process was hardly finished. Once she sent her edits back, there would be another few weeks of reviewing the edits. I liked my male character, Donovan Anderson. Like the real man he was based on, he was also a financial advisor.

Still, Brendan was more desirable than the character I'd created this time.

He was the real deal, and tonight he was cooking for me.

Brendan lived in neighborhood with gorgeous townhomes. His was on a corner, making it easy to find. I parked near his black Audi and rang his doorbell.

He opened the door, dressed in another polo shirt and jeans. I determined this was his usual casual attire. I liked seeing him dressed down for the weekend.

He swept his hand elegantly, bidding me inside his home. "Welcome, my lady."

"Thank you." *My lady. I liked that.*

Brendan's house was definitely a bachelor pad, but I liked his tastes. He had the typical large screen television in his living room that most guys loved. He opted for a black suede sectional that had numerous pillows each with an African inspired pattern. I glanced around to find framed photos of women who shared Brendan's skin complexion and eyes.

"Your family?" I pointed towards the framed portraits.

"Yes, that's my mother and my maternal grandmother. They passed away about seven years apart. Both strokes. It's one of the reasons why I'm really self-conscious about my health."

That made sense. I peered up at the women again, hoping they approved of me. I glanced around, thinking his home really represented his laid back personality.

"Come, you can have a seat at the table. I will be serving shortly."

I took that moment to acknowledge the smells wafting from the kitchen. "Mmm, it smells delicious. I can't wait to taste it."

Brendan pulled out a chair at the table which was already set. My eyes fell on a centerpiece with several small lit candles.

This is by far the most romantic dinner I'd ever been invited to.

I waited for signs of doubts, but none came. I was going to enjoy this time with Brendan and enjoy the meal cooked by his hands.

I watched over the kitchen counter, trying to glimpse what he had prepared. "You don't need my help?"

He shook his head, "Nope. This is me treating you. I just want you to enjoy." He walked out with a basket of what appeared to be covered cornbread. Next, he brought out salads.

"I made a balsamic vinaigrette. Want to try?"

"Sure." If Brendan was trying to impress me, I was thoroughly smitten, and we hadn't even gotten to the main course yet. The salad was fresh and the cornbread was delish. "You made these too?"

He grinned. "Everything is from scratch. I started this morning."

"Wow."

"Ready for the main course?"

"Bring it on."

He set a steaming serving bowl in the middle of the table. When he pulled the top off, to my delight, the meal included large shrimp on top of creamy grits.

I eyed him. "Who told you my favorite meal was shrimp and grits?"

He chuckled. "I promise, no one leaked that information to me."

"If you say so." I scooped the shrimp and grits onto my plate and began to taste. "Oh this is scrumptious. You definitely need to consider being a chef for real."

"I will settle for cooking for you for now."

We enjoyed the rest of the meal, topping it off with one of my aunt's pies, of course. I'd remembered to bring the apple pie. Brendan added whip cream to both of our slices, making dessert a perfect complement to the meal.

Brendan asked, "What do you think?"

"I think you are fabulous." The words spilled out of my mouth before I could stop them. I added. "And I'm looking forward to becoming great friends and..."

He finished my sentence. "Much more."

"Yes. I attend Victory Gospel Church on Sundays. You want to come?"

He smiled. "Sure, I would love to meet you for service."

"My mom and Aunt Linda will probably be there. And they may act up a bit."

"I look forward to getting to know them too." He stood and reached for my hand. "I have a good feeling we're heading in the right direction."

I stood. "I agree."

This time when Brendan leaned down, our lips touched.

And I reveled in my own sweet romance.

About the Author

Tyora Moody writes romantic suspense and mysteries with sassy women sleuths. When Tyora isn't working for a literary client, she enjoys reading, spending time with family, binge-watching crime shows, catching a movie on the big screen, and traveling. To contact Tyora about book club discussions, visit her online at TyoraMoody.com.

www.ingramcontent.com/pod-product-compliance
Lightning Source LLC
Chambersburg PA
CBHW031937240626
47153CB00003B/766